"We'll get through this," Duke said.

Oregon glanced at him. "I know we will."

She watched him stack boxes along the back of the truck. He turned, keeping his head ducked because the truck didn't allow for his height. "You don't sound convinced."

"I'm trying," she assured him.

He jumped down, landing next to her. He touched her cheek with a large, calloused hand, gently forcing her to look at him. That meant looking into blue eyes that were as clear as a summer sky. She could lose herself in his eyes, in the promises she saw in them. His mouth curved in an easy smile as he leaned a little toward her.

"You need to start believing." He spoke softly. "Because I won't let us fail as a family."

Family. But they weren't one, she thought to tell him, but she couldn't form the words.

For a moment she was lost because she'd honestly thought he meant to kiss her when he leaned close. And she couldn't let that happen.

Brenda Minton lives in the Ozarks with her husband, children, cats, dogs and strays. She is a pastor's wife, Sunday school teacher, coffee addict and sleep deprived. Not in that order. Her dream to be an author for Harlequin started somewhere in the pages of a romance novel about a young American woman stranded in a Spanish castle. Her dreams came true and twenty-plus books later, she is an author hoping to inspire young girls to dream.

Books by Brenda Minton

Love Inspired

Martin's Crossing

A Rancher for Christmas
The Rancher Takes a Bride

Cooper Creek

Christmas Gifts
"Her Christmas Cowboy"
The Cowboy's Holiday Blessing
The Bull Rider's Baby
The Rancher's Secret Wife
The Cowboy's Healing Ways
The Cowboy Lawman
The Cowboy's Christmas Courtship
The Cowboy's Reunited Family
Single Dad Cowboy

Visit the Author Profile page at Harlequin.com for more titles

 LOVE INSPIRED BOOKS

Recycling programs
for this product may
not exist in your area.

ISBN-13: 978-0-373-81834-1

The Rancher Takes a Bride

Copyright © 2015 by Brenda Minton

www.Harlequin.com

Printed in U.S.A.

The Rancher Takes a Bride

Brenda Minton

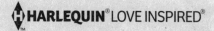

The eyes of your understanding being enlightened; that ye may know what is the hope of his calling, and what the riches of the glory of his inheritance in the saints.
—*Ephesians* 1:18

In memory of my father-in-law, Jacob Minton.
Real men read romance, and he read every book.

Chapter One

Spring in Martin's Crossing, Texas, meant one thing to Oregon Jeffries. It meant another year of working up the courage to do the right thing. As she pushed petunias into the soil of the planter outside her shop, Oregon's All Things, she thought about taking that step to make things right.

"Mom, you're going to kill it pushing it in like that." Her daughter, Lilly, appeared next to her, peering in at the plant.

She had a point. The petunia looked a little droopy from the handling it had received. One stem even appeared to be broken. Oregon pushed hair back from her face and patted the soil more gently.

"You're right. I should be more careful."

"Do you want me to finish them later?"

Lilly, at twelve, was willing to do almost anything to help. Except maybe laundry.

"No, I'll do them. Don't you have a job to get to?"

Lilly glanced across the street, her blue eyes focusing on Duke's No Bar and Grill. It was a long, low building with wood siding and a covered front deck running the length of the restaurant.

"Yeah, Duke said I could sweep up and water flowers. But I know you don't like me working for him."

"I didn't say…" Well, maybe she had said something about wishing her daughter would find other jobs. But Lilly wanted a horse, and they'd made a deal that she had to work and earn the money to pay for the horse and the upkeep. As a single mom, Oregon couldn't handle the expense of a horse. Plus, she thought her daughter would appreciate it more if she helped pay for the animal.

The townspeople in Martin's Crossing had pitched in and given Lilly odd jobs. Each time she got paid, Lilly put most of the money in the jar she kept hidden in her room. And she put a portion in the offering at church.

Duke Martin, owner of Duke's No Bar and Grill, had been giving Lilly various jobs since he learned of her quest to buy a horse. He'd even offered to help her pick a good, well-broke horse when she had all the money saved.

"You can go to Duke's. Just don't be a nuisance," she warned.

Lilly kissed her cheek, and Oregon nearly cried. Her daughter no longer had to stand on tiptoes; instead, Lilly leaned down a bit because she'd outgrown Oregon over the winter.

"Thanks, Mom."

Oregon nodded and went back to her flowers.

As she reached for another petunia, tires screeched, followed by shouting and then a sickening thud. Oregon turned, screaming as she saw her daughter fall to the asphalt. Everything slowed. Except her heart, which beat rapidly in her chest as she stood frozen on the sidewalk.

The driver of the car jumped out. Duke ran down the steps of the restaurant. Oregon couldn't move. Couldn't breathe. She heard Duke yell at her, then everything returned to normal speed.

There were people everywhere. Where did they all come from? Oregon felt a hand on her arm, a voice comforting her. "She's going to be okay. You need to go to her."

It was Joe, the vagrant who had appeared in town last winter. He held her arm and walked with her to Lilly's crumpled body. Duke knelt next to her daughter. His large body hovered, his fingers touching Lilly's neck, then her wrist.

"Don't move," he whispered when she tried to sit up. And then he saw Oregon. "Your mom is here. Stay still, sweetheart. Stay still."

Oregon knelt next to her baby girl, brushing dark hair back from her pale face, noticing the bruises on her temple and cheek. Lilly opened her eyes and whispered that it hurt. Tears were streaming down her cheeks. Duke stopped Oregon from scooping her up and holding her close.

"You can't do that, Oregon." He yelled for someone to bring a blanket.

Oregon saw that her daughter was trembling and pale.

"Oregon, hold it together." Duke's voice whispered in her ear. "Talk to her."

She nodded and leaned in, unsure of what to say. Duke's hand was on her back. Oregon wanted to sob. But she didn't. Instead, she took Lilly's hand and held it. "The ambulance is on the way, honey. We'll get you help. You'll be okay."

A man shouted that he hadn't seen her. That she'd come out of nowhere. Duke stood up and headed for the driver of the car. Six feet eight inches of Duke Martin had the man backing away, holding his hands up.

Oregon heard him tell the driver to sit and save his explanations. Right now they were going to take care of the child he'd hit. Her child. Oregon's hand shook as she smoothed her daughter's hair back from her face once more.

If Duke only knew, Oregon thought. She kissed her daughter's cheek. "It's going to be okay. I hear the ambulance."

"Mommy, it hurts."

"Can you tell me where it hurts, Lilly?" Duke once again took charge. He'd been an army medic in Afghanistan.

"Everywhere," Lilly answered. "My leg. And my head. My stomach."

"Do you remember where you were going?" he asked.

"To school," she responded.

Though she had tried to fight it, the tears overtook Oregon. She felt strong hands on her shoulders. Joe pulled her to her feet and led her away. The ambulance pulled up, and Duke spoke with quiet authority as they assessed her daughter.

"I need to be with her." Oregon tried to pull away from Joe.

"No, you need to stand here and let them do their job," he insisted, his voice soft but firm. "Stay here with me and when they're ready to leave, you can give her a kiss and tell her you'll meet her at the hospital."

"But I should go with her..."

"You can't." Joe led her toward the stretcher holding her daughter. Her baby. She tried to pull away from Joe, but he held tight. "Oregon, take a deep breath and tell our girl she'll be okay."

Our girl. The words registered faintly. Everyone in town considered Lilly their girl. People here loved them, cared about them. It was one of the reasons she'd stayed in Martin's Crossing. Because for the first time in her life, she felt as if she truly belonged. Though she had wanted it more for her daughter than herself, that sense of belonging somewhere.

Joe led her back to Lilly and held her hand as she kissed her daughter on the forehead, said a quick prayer and told her they would meet her at the hospital.

"Mommy, I'll be okay." Lilly's voice shook as she said the words.

"Of course you'll be okay," Oregon managed in a voice that remained steady. Because she was the mom. She would make sure her daughter was okay. God couldn't take her baby. They needed each other too much.

As she stepped back, Joe touched Lilly's brow. He smiled at her and whispered that she'd be home soon, and they'd talk more about that horse. Oregon wanted to tell him not to make promises. Oregon knew how easily they were broken.

Duke stood next to the ambulance as Lilly was loaded on. He spoke to the paramedics. Then he nodded and said something to Lilly. And Oregon stood there, letting him take charge because she couldn't move. Couldn't think.

Her body began to shake as the ambulance pulled away. "I have to go." Oregon headed for her shop and apartment. She had to find her purse, her keys…

"Oregon, wait."

She turned to see Duke striding across the street toward her. Joe came with him. She looked from Joe with his weathered face, gray hair and easy smile to Duke, a giant of a man with sandy-brown hair starting to grow out from the buzz cut he'd had, unshaved face and piercing blue eyes.

"What?" Her voice trembled, and for a scary moment everything faded. She took a deep breath and her vision cleared.

Duke's features softened as he looked at her.

"I'm driving." He had his truck keys out. "Lock up your shop and let's go."

"I can drive. You really don't have to."

He let out a long sigh. "Oregon, don't argue with me. You're in no condition to drive. I'm taking you."

She nodded and hurried inside, finding her purse and her keys, leaving the petunias on the stoop to be planted later. As she walked out the front door, locking it behind her, Joe was telling Duke he'd like to ride along. Duke looked to Oregon, and she nodded.

Joe was little more than a stranger, a homeless man who had worked for Duke and moved into a small house down the street. But he was a good man, and Lilly adored him.

Today she needed these two men. And she needed for Lilly to be okay. She needed to know that God heard her prayers.

She needed the strength of Duke's arms

as he walked her to his waiting truck. Those big arms made her rethink everything. It was time to tell the truth. Her heart ached, worrying about her daughter, about their future and Duke's reaction to the news she would tell him.

Duke risked a cautious look at Oregon to make sure she was holding it together. She'd been unusually quiet on the ride to Austin. Joe, who sat next to her, was also quiet. He saw that Oregon's eyes were closed, and her lips were moving as she prayed.

He didn't know much about her, but he did know she attended Martin's Crossing Community Church. He'd seen her there the few times he'd darkened the door. Now he knew she was a praying woman. He also knew that she had a mom who liked to stir up trouble and who wasn't too fond of Oregon's religion.

He'd like to reclaim his own faith, but he and God were having some issues about prayers he'd said for kids in Afghanistan. He shook his head, not wanting to focus on that, not right now with Lilly on her way to the hospital.

He reached for Oregon's hand and squeezed it. "She's going to be okay."

"I know. I know." Oregon wiped away the tears that streamed down her cheeks. "She was talking. That's a good sign. Isn't it?"

"Yes, always a good sign."

Anger suddenly flashed in her eyes. Funny, he'd thought they were hazel; now he realized they were the warmest shade of gray possible. "Don't tell me what you think I want to hear, Duke. You were a medic. I want your opinion."

"A medic, not a doctor. And kids aren't exactly my area of expertise."

"Duke, please."

He slowed for a stoplight. "Only a mile to the hospital."

"What are you trying to hide?"

"I'm not hiding anything. I'm just trying to decide the best answer because I don't want to say the wrong thing."

"Tell me she's going to be okay," she sobbed.

Yeah, that's exactly what he was avoiding. "I think she had broken bones and possibly some internal injuries. I'm going by my own assessment and the paramedics' conversation as they loaded her in the ambulance."

Oregon nodded, the conversation ending in nervous silence. Joe patted Oregon's leg and said that he knew one thing with certainty; that God would take care of Lilly. Duke didn't say that he'd seen a lot of prayers go unanswered during his time in Afghanistan.

"Here we are." He pulled his truck into the hospital parking lot and found a space close to the emergency room. He exited and then waited for Oregon.

Something happened in that moment as he watched and waited for her to get out. It was like the past crashing into the future, and he didn't know what it meant. It was a flashback of laughing with a dark-haired girl who had just won her first cash prize on a barrel horse she'd trained herself. With a shake of his head he cleared the memory.

Sitting in his truck, Oregon visibly pulled herself together before she stepped out. The wind whipped her hair and wrapped her prairie skirt around her legs. Joe waited for them on the other side. The three of them walked toward the emergency room entrance. As they got closer, Oregon's steps slowed, faltering. Duke took her hand and looked down at her. Her eyes met his and it seemed familiar.

He shook it off. The memory wasn't real.

But the pain in her eyes was. He squeezed her hand. "She'll be okay."

"I'm taking your word for that." Her voice trembled on the words.

Duke led her through the automatic doors to a desk, where a receptionist smiled up at them. Joe stood on her other side, his hand on her back.

"We're here with Lilly Jeffries, brought in by ambulance from Martin's Crossing," Duke told the woman who had already started searching her computer.

"Are you parents or legal guardians?" the receptionist asked, barely looking up at them.

"I'm her mother," Oregon replied.

"She's being examined right now." The woman behind the desk pushed paperwork on a clipboard across the counter. "If you could fill this out."

"I want to see my daughter." Oregon's voice didn't shake. She looked at the woman, her eyes fierce, the way a mother's eyes should be.

Not that Duke had any real experience with mothers. His own had skipped out on them right before his tenth birthday. They hadn't seen her since the day she hopped in her car and took off.

Oregon wasn't that kind of mom.

The receptionist nodded, and her features

softened. "Green ward, room C. Take the paperwork with you."

"Thank you."

Duke reached for her hand, a strangely familiar gesture. He'd ignored this woman for the past year. He'd been busy with his diner. She'd been busy getting her own business off the ground. She hadn't seemed to want more from him than an occasional take-out meal. Come to think of it, she'd rarely stepped foot in the diner. She'd always sent Lilly to get their food.

Why was he thinking about this now, as she walked next to him, her hand tightly gripping his? Joe walked on her other side, quiet, staid. The older man had settled in a few months back and seemed content to stay awhile in Martin's Crossing.

They reached the room with the open glass door. Inside, a doctor stood next to Lilly, his smile easy, his gestures not those of a man in the middle of an emergency. He waved them inside.

"You must be Mom. We've been asking for you. After we settled on the fact that it isn't Saturday, and she wasn't on her way to school when the bus hit her." The doctor smiled down at his patient. "We're going to do a CT scan of that head, and then we'll do some X-rays."

The doctor motioned Oregon out of the room and followed close behind her. Duke went with her. Joe stayed with Lilly, who grimaced in pain as she told him something they couldn't hear after the doctor slid that glass door closed.

"You're her dad?" the doctor asked. Duke shook his head.

"No. I just drove her mom up here." He glanced down at the woman next to him, her lower lip between her teeth, her worried gaze on the girl inside that room.

"You can stay," she whispered, still not looking at him.

The doctor looked from Oregon to Duke, gave a curt nod and continued. "We're going to run some tests. She has some abdominal tenderness. I'm sure we've got a fracture in her left leg. We'll know more after X-rays."

"She'll be okay?" Oregon finally looked away from her daughter and made eye contact with the doctor.

"She'll be fine. She's not going to be happy when she realizes what a cast will do to her summer activities, but hopefully we can have her back on two good legs very soon."

"Can I go back in now?"

Sliding the door back open, the doctor said, "You have a few minutes, then you can wait in here for us while we run the tests."

She nodded as she walked away, leaving Duke with the strangest feeling in the pit of his stomach as he watched the less than animated form of Lilly on that hospital bed. Joe stepped out of the room to join him.

"She'll be okay." Joe said it like he was comforting Duke.

"Of course she will. Her mom is here now."

Joe gave him a puzzled look and shook his head. "You going in there?"

No, he wasn't. He had done his part. He'd been shaken to his core when he'd seen that car speeding down the street, seen her freeze in her tracks as the sedan screeched to a stop too late. It could have been worse, he'd told himself. Much worse.

He shook his head, not wanting to replay it in his mind again. What he needed was…a cup of coffee. He made his excuses and headed down the hall. Joe started to follow.

Duke put his hand out to stop the older man from tagging along, giving advice he didn't want or need. "Give me a minute alone."

"She's okay, Duke."

"I know that."

He knew she was okay. He didn't know if *he* was, though. He'd nearly put the nightmares to rest in the last year or so. He'd been almost back to normal. But now faces were flashing through his memory. Names he'd almost forgotten were surfacing. A man didn't forget those young men, their names, their stories.

He put his dollar in the vending machine and raised his hand, ready to pound his fist against the glass front, but then he stopped himself. His chest ached, and each breath had to work its way from lungs that seemed to be closing up.

A hand touched his back, small and gentle. He didn't turn. He knew that it was Oregon. He inhaled her presence, the soft scent of wildflowers.

"Are you okay?" she asked.

He nodded, slowing his breaths, feeling his heart return to normal. Yeah, he was fine.

"We have to talk," she said so softly he almost didn't hear.

But he'd known this moment was coming.

Chapter Two

Oregon stood in front of Duke, his features chiseled in stone but somehow beautiful with his bright blue eyes, wide, smiling mouth and golden skin. He'd been just as beautiful thirteen years ago. She'd been eighteen. He'd been barely twenty. It had been the year her mom married a Texas rancher who raised quarter horses and didn't mind Oregon trying to be a cowgirl.

Now she had to tell him what she'd come here to tell him. It'd been a year since she'd first arrived in Martin's Crossing. At first she hadn't told him, because she needed time. Needed to make sure he was a person she wanted in her daughter's life. She wanted to know that Lilly would have someone she could depend on. Someone who wouldn't walk away, who wouldn't let her down.

"Oregon?" His voice was cold. His tone hard.

He knew.

"It's about Lilly."

"What about Lilly?"

"Lilly is…" She looked past him, down the empty hall. Where were all the people who would interrupt, keeping her from having this difficult conversation?

He took her hand and led her to a consultation room that was empty. She balked at the door. "We can't just walk in there."

"We can and will." He pulled her inside.

Once the door was closed, he pointed to a yellow vinyl chair. She sat and he stood in front of the door like a bouncer at a club. Blocking her from running? No. He stood because he had too much energy to sit. Sometimes in the early-morning hours she saw him running through the streets of Martin's Crossing. Sometimes she saw him at night. Outrunning his nightmares, she thought.

These were some of the many things she'd learned about him since moving to town. Thirteen years ago, she hadn't known much. She'd known he was a young man with a lot of anger who partied too hard. He'd team roped with his brother, Jake. He'd bought her a cheeseburger, and she'd laughed when he wiped ketchup off her chin, right before he kissed her.

"So, Oregon Jeffries. Tell me everything."

"I think you know."

"Enlighten me."

"We met in a small town outside Stephenville, Texas, when I was eighteen. Nine months later, I had Lilly. When I first came to Martin's Crossing, I thought you'd recognize me. But you didn't. I was just the mother of the girl who swept the porch of your diner. You didn't remember me. Not a flicker of recognition or a question about who we were." She shrugged, waiting for him to say something.

He brushed a hand across his face and shook his head. "I'm afraid to admit I have a few blank spots in my memory. Bad choices in my youth. You probably know that already."

"It's become clear since I got to town and you didn't recognize me."

"Or my daughter?"

His words froze her heart. She trembled, and she didn't want to be weak. Not today. Not when her daughter was somewhere in this hospital having tests done. Today she needed strength and the truth. Because some people thought the truth could set her free. She worried it would only mean losing her daughter to this man who had already made himself a hero to Lilly.

What if he wasn't the man they needed him to be? Oregon wanted to stop the cycle of broken promises, broken relationships. She wanted Lilly to have a solid foundation that didn't shift and move on the whim of an adult.

"She's my daughter." He repeated it again, his voice soft with wonder.

"Yes, she's your daughter." She whispered the words into the small room. A Gideon bible had been placed on the table between two chairs. A lamp in the corner offered soft light. In this room, lives changed. People were given the worst news. People received options.

In this room, Duke Martin learned he was a father.

"Why didn't you try to contact me?" He sat down heavily, stretching his long legs in front of him. "Did you think I wouldn't want to know?"

"I knew from friends that you had a problem with alcohol. And then I found out you joined the army. Duke, I was used to my mother dragging me along from relationship to relationship. She was with men who were abusive, who were alcoholics, and a few who were okay. I didn't want that for my daughter."

Oregon's own father hadn't stayed. He'd been a nameless man who walked out on them. And then there had been her mother's countless marriages, with Oregon never being given a choice in the matter.

"You should have told me," Duke stormed in a quiet voice, respectful of this place. She'd learned something about him in the past year. She'd learned that looks could be deceiving. He looked like Goliath. But beneath his large exterior, he was good and kind.

He kept his power carefully leashed, his temper controlled, his voice even in tone. He leaned forward in the chair, brushing his hand through his short hair.

"You've been in town over a year. You should have told me sooner," he repeated.

"Maybe I should have, but I needed to know you, to be sure about you, before I put you in my daughter's life."

"Maybe?" He erupted in quiet anger. "*Maybe* you should have told me Lilly is mine? What if something had…"

She shook her head. "No, don't go there."

"You kept her from me," he said in a quieter voice.

"You have to understand. I was eighteen and alone and making stupid decisions. And now I'm a mom who has to make sure her daughter isn't going to be hurt. I have to make sure the man I bring into her life isn't going to walk out on her."

"I do not walk out."

"I know. And I *was* going to tell you. I just didn't know how."

"You could have told me years ago. A letter, even a short note, would have been nice."

"You left." Another person in her life who had left. Not that she'd expected him to stay. He'd been a day, a smile, a moment. She'd been a kid who'd made bad choices in her search for love.

"You know for sure…" he started to ask, but his words trailed off.

"I know without a doubt. There are no other possibilities."

He studied her for a few seconds. She met his gaze head-on because she had to be strong. "Why did you change your mind and decide to bring her to Martin's Crossing?"

Of course he would want to know that. She

would tell him why, but not today. She couldn't tell him everything, not in one crazy, overly emotional day. "I knew she needed you."

The simple answer was the truth. It was enough for now.

She wasn't telling him everything but for Duke, it was enough for one day. He had a daughter. For the past year Lilly had bounced in and out of his diner. She'd swept his floors. She'd talked to him about the kind of horse she wanted. She'd looked up at him with those blue eyes that were so much like his, he should have seen himself in her. He should have seen it. He should have recognized Oregon.

He rubbed the top of his head and stared at the woman he'd let down, mother of the girl he'd let down. He'd become his mother. Man, he wanted to pound something. He needed to get on his bike and take a long ride through Texas. But unlike Sylvia Martin, his mother, he would come back. But he wouldn't walk away from this hospital, from Lilly or Oregon.

He looked at her. Her dark hair framed a face that was delicate and shifted from cute to pretty with a smile. She shrugged slim shoulders. "Maybe you should have remembered but you said it yourself, there are a lot of holes in your memory."

Yeah, a lot of holes. Blackouts. Days lost. He reached into his pocket and felt that coin he carried, a reminder of how long he'd been sober. Two years and counting.

"I'm sorry," he said as he made eye contact with the woman sitting across from him.

"I'm sorry, too. I know she needs you."

There were so many ways he could react to that. He could be angry, but what would that get him? She had wanted to protect her daughter. He couldn't blame her for that.

"So I guess I passed the test," he finally said.

"Of course you do." She stood, her eyes darting away from him to the door. "We should go. I don't want her to be alone too long."

"No, of course not." She would never be alone again. He would see to that. "Does she know?"

"That you're her dad? No."

"We have to tell her."

They walked out into the hall and headed back to the emergency room. "Yes, I know."

"What does she know?"

"That I was young and made a mistake. But that *she* isn't a mistake."

"Man, Oregon, I should have been there. I should have been in her life."

"I didn't mean for this to happen." Her voice faltered.

"You weren't in this alone. And you aren't alone now. We need to get married." The words slipped out quickly, without giving them a lot of thought.

She stopped. He took a few more steps and then turned to face her. She was barely five feet tall. Her dark hair was long and soft. Her gray eyes had flecks of green in this light. Had he just proposed to her?

"No." And with that simple answer, she kept walking.

He froze under the bright fluorescent lights, voices of people heading in their direction. Ahead of him Oregon kept walking. He was so tall that he only had to take a few steps and he was next to her.

"Why not?"

"Because this isn't love. It was attraction once. Now we're two strangers, and that isn't enough for a marriage."

"Our daughter deserves—"

She cut him off with an angry glare. "Don't

tell me what she deserves. She deserves a home and people who love her. People who stay."

"Right, but we have to think about our daughter."

"Mine," she cried out, her eyes widening in fear. "She's *my* daughter."

"I'm not going to take her from you." He said it as calmly as he could, in the voice he used to soothe startled horses.

"No, but you could take her heart. She already loves you."

"Oregon, this isn't a competition."

They kept walking back to the ward with green walls, and rooms with glass doors, curtains for privacy and hushed voices. Oregon stopped, leaning against the wall a few short feet from the nurses' station.

"Duke, she needs you. That's why we're here. Right now I'm emotional and not thinking straight. My main concern is for her, that she's safe and she's going to be okay. Marriage to you, though, is not in my plans."

"We won't discuss it today. You're right. She needs us with her now."

He could understand her reluctance to marry. He hadn't seen too much about marriage that he admired. But his brother Jake, the last guy he thought would fall, seemed to be taken with the idea. Jake and Breezy had fallen in love with each other, with the twin nieces they all shared, and the rest had been history. In their current newlywed phase of soft looks, sweet smiles and easy embraces, it was impossible to be around them for long.

Duke avoided them as much as possible. He didn't need to see their version of happily-ever-after.

He'd rather stay at his old house, working on the wiring that needed updating, the plumbing that sometimes groaned with the effort of pushing water to the faucets.

A house for a family, Jake had teased when Duke started the remodel. And now he had a family. True, Oregon didn't want any part of making them one. But Duke would be a dad to Lilly. He wouldn't let her argue him out of that.

They entered the room as a nurse was settling Lilly back in, covering her with heated blankets and tucking in the edges.

The nurse smiled at her patient. "Told you they'd be right back."

Oregon leaned to kiss her daughter's cheek.

Their daughter. Duke hung back, trying hard not to let this moment get the best of him. This shouldn't be the first time he saw her as his daughter. There should have been a lifetime of moments. A newborn in a hospital, first steps, first words, first day of school. Yeah, he'd missed out on a lot.

He wanted to be angry with Oregon. He was angry, not just with her, with himself. He hadn't been the kind of man a woman would turn to.

This girl could have pulled him back to where he needed to be.

She still could.

For the moment he stood on the sidelines and watched as the nurse checked IV lines, as Oregon spoke in soft whispers and then as Joe reentered the room with a cup of coffee. Why in the world did this drama include Joe?

How did a man adjust to suddenly being a dad?

The doctor walked through the sliding door. He looked at his chart, looked up and smiled at Lilly, then at Oregon. He didn't look at Duke or Joe, because they were just the extras in this scene.

The doctor pulled back the blanket, touched Lilly's toes on her left foot, rested a hand on the splinted leg. "Well, we have a minor concussion, and she's very fortunate it wasn't worse. No internal bleeding, for which we're thankful. And then this broken leg that we're going to set. She'll be down for about six weeks, then back to work earning money for that horse."

"Oh, she told you." Oregon smiled down at her daughter.

"Yes, she did. She also told me you have stairs. She's not going to have an easy time on stairs with the cast and crutches."

"We'll figure something out," Duke cut in. Oregon shot him a look that clearly told him to stay out of her business.

Thing is, her business had become his. He gave her a look that he hoped told her he wasn't going to back down and pretend this didn't matter. He ignored the daggers Oregon shot at him from eyes damp with unshed tears and smiled at Lilly. She smiled back with a smile he should have recognized.

Yeah, this mattered.

After it was decided Lilly would spend the night in the hospital, Duke took Joe home, then headed for the ranch. Or his section of the nearly twelve hundred acres that made up the Circle M.

He bypassed Jake's place and drove down

the dirt road to his house. The two-story home had a pillared front porch and a veranda that ran across the second floor. It had been a showplace years ago when his grandfather had been alive. And then it had been abandoned and had started to fall apart. Posts on the porch had needed to be replaced, along with the roof, siding and many of the windows.

Beyond this house was a caretaker's cottage, with two bedrooms and a sunny living room. He'd lived in the cottage for six months, since he'd begun the initial repairs to the main house. Today he'd had an idea.

The cottage was one story, no steps and no porches. Just a nice little rock house with a front door, a back patio and a few flower gardens. Perfect for Oregon and Lilly. Not that he thought it would be that easy. He could already hear Oregon's objections in his head.

A truck pulled up the drive as he sat there looking at the cottage. He groaned as he took a quick look in his rearview mirror. The last thing he needed was big brother time. But sooner or later it would have to take place.

He got out of his truck as Jake parked. Jake stepped out of his own vehicle with an easy smile on his face. Jake had always been the one taking charge of their family, making the hard decisions. Duke guessed it hadn't been all Jake's fault. Duke hadn't been that much younger; he'd just found other ways to deal with life. He'd been out partying, team roping and running from the pain their mother had caused them all.

Jake had grown more and more resentful, taking the burden of raising the Martins and keeping the ranch in the black.

"Saw you drive by," Jake said as he shoved his hands deep into the pockets of his jeans and rocked on the heels of his boots. He looked from the house to Duke. "Is Lilly okay?"

Duke stared at the cottage and avoided looking at his brother. He guessed that Jake really wanted to ask if he was sober. He'd passed seven bars and three liquor stores on his way home. He hadn't stopped at one of them. Hadn't even been tempted. That said something.

"Yeah, she'll be okay. Broken leg, concussion, a bruised spleen."

"Where are they?"

"Still at the hospital. I thought they might be able to stay here. More room and no stairs."

"Right." Silence stretched on, and finally Jake smiled a little. "She's yours, isn't she?"

Duke nodded. "Yeah, she's mine."

"Do we need a DNA test?"

That made him mad. "She isn't here to get anything from me. The last thing she wanted to do was tell me I had a daughter. But today seemed to be the day."

He had a daughter. The idea settled inside him, making him angry and glad and hurt, all at the same time. Jake's grinning wasn't going to help. He shot his brother a warning look and stomped off. Jake gave him a few minutes to cool his heels before following him inside the cottage.

"This isn't something you keep from a man," he told Jake as he rummaged through the kitchen cabinets.

"No, I reckon it isn't." Jake opened the fridge and pulled out a package of moldy lunch meat. "Wouldn't hurt you to get a wife."

"I proposed. She isn't interested."

Jake laughed. "Proposed? What did you say, 'Gee, I guess we should get married'? You're the ladies' man. I expect better from you."

Duke laughed, and it loosened something inside him, something that had been tight as a clock and ready to spring loose. "I expect better from myself. I guess if a guy was going

to have a kid, he'd expect to remember that
he had her."

He brushed a hand across the top of his
head. Jake watched, hip against the counter,
cowboy hat pulled low.

"Well, now you know. Guess what you gotta
do is decide how to go forward from here."

"I go forward as a dad. End of story."

Jake shrugged, looking comfortable in his
own skin. Duke had always thought of himself as the comfortable one. Today cool and
unflustered belonged to Jake.

"Might call Charlie and get advice."

"I don't need your attorney."

"Fine, you'll figure it out." Jake gave the
easy answer as he stepped away from the cab-
inet.

Yes, he would find a way to be Lilly's dad.
He guessed he'd start by getting her that horse
she wanted.

And he'd have to figure out his relationship
with Oregon.

Chapter Three

"Where are we going?" Lilly asked as they got closer to Martin's Crossing. She was in Duke's truck, leaning against Oregon. Her leg in the bright pink knee-to-foot cast was stretched out, nearly touching Duke's leg as he drove.

He'd showed up at the hospital that morning with the news that he would be driving them home. Oregon had allowed it because she didn't have a car there and because he was Lilly's dad.

She'd spent a lot of sleepless nights thinking about how everything would change when she told him. It was no longer the Lilly and Oregon show. Duke was now a part of their lives. They couldn't go back. In some strange way they were now a family unit. They would have to figure out how it changed things, what it meant for the future. She knew he deserved this, to be in Lilly's life.

Oregon knew it would hurt in ways she hadn't expected. Because the young cowboy she'd met thirteen years ago had been a force to be reckoned with. He'd had a charming smile, too much confidence and a way with words. He'd melted her resistance. She'd wanted love. She'd wanted forever. All from a man she'd known for a weekend.

Looking back, she knew how wrong that had been.

But present-day Duke was more of a concern. This man now had shadows in blue eyes that once had been carefree, full of laughter. This man now knew how to be a friend. How to be there for the people he cared about.

It didn't take a genius to know her heart could be broken all over again if she wasn't careful. Lilly moved, repositioning herself, bringing Oregon out of her own thoughts.

"Yes, Duke, where are we going?" She repeated her daughter's question.

He'd been pretty mysterious since he showed up in the hospital room carrying a bouquet of flowers with a half-dozen balloons attached. It took up the entire back-seat of his truck.

"We're going to the ranch. I want to show you all something," he answered. Once again mysterious, but this time with a hint of a smile.

"We should go back to our place so Lilly can rest." Oregon hooked an arm around her daughter and Lilly snuggled close, probably drifting back to sleep again.

"Yes, rest is a good idea," Duke answered vaguely and kept on driving.

They turned onto the road to the Circle M. The paved road ended at Jake's house and became dirt. Fences lined both sides of the road. They drove past Duke's house and then past a barn. In the field cattle grazed, and near the barn a few horses raised their heads and watched the truck drive by.

"This is pretty," Lilly mumbled, lifting her head to look around.

"Yes, it is." Duke pulled up to a stone cottage.

"Duke, what is this?" Oregon felt a twinge of uncertainty bordering on fear.

She'd been in Martin's Crossing long enough to know he wasn't going to let her call all of the shots now that he knew about Lilly. A part of her wanted to tell him to back off. Another part of her wanted him to pretend nothing had changed.

"Let's get out," he said. He opened the truck door and reached in the backseat for pink crutches, handing them to Lilly. "Come on, kiddo."

Lilly, suddenly wide awake, grabbed the crutches and allowed him to help her out. No, it wouldn't take Oregon's daughter long to adjust to this new situation. Lilly smiled up at him and he leaned, giving her a loose hug. He was everything that any little girl would dream of in a dad. Especially Oregon's little girl, who had watched with envy when other little girls sat on their daddy's shoulders or rode bikes down the street together. Oregon knew that type of envy because she'd felt it often growing up.

"Coming?" Duke glanced back inside the truck, and Oregon nodded. Did she have a choice? Duke wasn't smiling. His mouth was a straight, unforgiving line. His jaw was set. No, he wasn't giving in.

She climbed out of the truck and met her daughter and Duke on the lawn, standing in front of the little stone house. "It's nice. This is where you've been staying while you remodeled the old house?"

"Yes, and it's where you're going to stay now. It doesn't have any steps. Even the porch is ground level. And the doors are wide."

Oregon stood there on the freshly mowed lawn, speechless. A black-and-white dog came down the drive. Of course it went right to Lilly, circling her, sniffing, brushy black tail wagging. "Lilly, be careful. Don't let him knock you down."

"She isn't going to knock me down, Mom." Lilly dropped one crutch and leaned down to pet the Border collie.

"But you can't fall. You have to be careful."

"She's careful." Duke spoke in a quiet voice of reason. She didn't want reasonable. Not right now. She picked up the crutch her daughter had dropped, and handed it to her. Lilly took it with a grimace and shoved it back under her arm.

When Oregon faced Duke, he nodded in Lilly's direction, stopping her from saying anything she'd regret. Oh, that didn't help. Reasonable, thoughtful, considerate male. How dare he?

"Oregon, I'm moving into the main house. I've been remodeling and it's close to finished. That means this cottage will be empty. It's quiet. It has room, and it doesn't have steps."

She left Lilly and Duke in the yard, Lilly sitting on a lawn chair, the dog practically climbing into her lap. Duke was answering a question about the horses he owned. Lilly had always been horse crazy. And dog crazy. They already had a dog at home. Joe had been taking care of it for them.

Oregon walked through the front door of the house, and her heart ached to claim this place as her own. It had windows that let in the breeze, freshly polished hardwood floors, a kitchen with white-painted cabinets and out the back door, a stone patio with a pretty teakwood table and a gas grill.

She strode out the back door. Alone, she stood on the stone patio and stared out at the grasslands of Texas. In the distance there were the hills that made Hill Country a destination for many travelers. It was late May, and the grass was green; wildflowers bloomed.

Footsteps told her she was no longer alone. Duke touched her back, his hand resting lightly. She had a sudden, overwhelming urge to lean into his embrace, to welcome the comfort he was offering. She wanted to soak up his scent, his strength. She turned to tell him this was too much, that she couldn't accept it, but when she turned, his arms went around her, and he pulled her close, bending to drop a kiss on the top of her head. It was what she'd dreamed of, and the last thing she wanted.

No, she didn't want to need him. But she couldn't make herself pull free from the embrace and all it offered.

"It's just a house, Oregon. It isn't a commitment. It isn't a ridiculous proposal offered on the spur of the moment. It's a place to live."

"It's too much," she tried to insist.

"You've raised my daughter alone for twelve years. I think I owe you a home to live in and more. Let me do this."

She nodded. "Thank you."

"Thank *you*. For bringing her here…and for telling me."

Behind them they heard the sound of crutches on the tile floor of the kitchen, then the squeak of the screen door. Oregon wiped her eyes and moved away from him to face her daughter. Lilly looked from Duke to Oregon, her eyes wide, suspicious.

"What's going on?" Lilly asked.

"Let's sit down out here and we'll talk," Oregon said with a lightness she was far from feeling.

"I'll get us a glass of tea," Duke offered.

Oregon nodded, accepting the offer as she

held out a chair for Lilly. Her daughter sat and was immediately joined by the dog.

"What's your dog's name, Duke?" Lilly asked.

"Daisy."

"Very manly," Lilly teased. Her smile was back, but she wouldn't offer it to Oregon.

Duke returned with three glasses of tea on a tray. "I stocked the fridge and cabinets."

"You didn't have to do that." Oregon didn't want him taking over, feeling as if he suddenly had to provide for them. Her shop, selling handmade creations of her own design, was doing quite well. She hadn't come here for support, for money. She just wanted her daughter to have what she'd never had. A real dad. A place to call home.

"I know I don't have to, Oregon. I wanted to make things easier for you."

"What if I'd said no?" she countered as she lifted the glass, condensation making the outside damp and cold.

"Okay, could we not start some kind of family disagreement," Lilly said. And then she looked at the two of them. "We're not a family."

Oregon bit down on her bottom lip and let her gaze slide to Duke. He was looking at her daughter, at *their* daughter. Oregon nodded when he looked to her for direction.

She had to do this.

"Lilly, we need to talk." Oregon began with those words, and Duke couldn't disagree. He didn't know any better way to start. But now that the words were said, he wondered if they should have given it more time. Maybe they should have prepared Lilly in some way. This was big news for a kid.

It had been pretty big news for him.

"Okay." Lilly sank her fingers into Daisy's black-and-white coat, and she looked at Duke as if he could make this any easier. He gave her what he hoped was an encouraging, hang-in-there smile.

"Duke and I knew each other a long time ago. We met at a rodeo when I was eighteen."

The words hung between them, and he felt like an acrobat on a tightrope, hanging precariously above this situation. Lilly continued to pet Daisy. She dropped her gaze to the dog with its tongue hanging out, a dog smile on her face. Daisy whined and moved in closer to Lilly, as if sensing that this wasn't good.

"How many years ago?" Lilly raised those blue eyes and looked from her mom to him.

"Almost thirteen years." Oregon spoke in a quiet voice, her gaze shifting from her daughter to him.

"Thirteen," Lilly whispered, her face pale, her hands clasping the dog, pulling her close. She buried her face against Daisy, and he had the sneaking suspicion she was hiding tears. His kid would do that. She'd hide it when she cried, and she'd fight anyone who said those were tears on her cheeks.

Duke sat there watching the girl who was his daughter. He didn't know what to say. He definitely didn't know what a dad would do in this situation.

He did know he'd knock down mountains for her. "Lilly, I'm sorry. If I'd known…"

She glared, eyes narrowed. "Sorry?" She shook her head, one tear sliding down her cheek. She brushed it away. "For what? For not telling me? For acting like my friend?"

Oregon opened her mouth; he was sure she meant to reprimand Lilly. He put a hand up, stopping the words. "She has a right to be angry."

He didn't have a manual on parenting, but he knew all about being an angry kid.

"Yeah, angry." Lilly said it like she was trying to find the emotion that fit. He guessed there was a lot of hurt. How much did they tell her? How much did they keep from her?

He looked to Oregon because she had the experience he was lacking. She moved her chair closer to her daughter. No, retract that, his daughter. Their daughter. He studied her face.

"Lilly, Duke didn't know. I waited too long and by the time I had found him, he'd joined the army and was on his way to Afghanistan."

"But you came here to tell him, and you didn't. Right?" Lilly swiped at angry tears chasing a trail down her cheeks. Duke brushed dampness from his own cheeks.

He hated that she was crying and that he didn't know how to fix this for her. He loved this kid and had from the first moment she bounded up the steps of the diner, asking for odd jobs to raise money for a horse. He'd given her a bridle for Christmas. She'd made him a card with a horse she drew. She'd signed it "with love, Lilly."

They'd had an immediate connection, he guessed. And he hadn't been smart enough to figure it out, to see the smile, the blue eyes, for what they were. His eyes. His sister's smile. Yeah, he saw it now. Lilly looked like his little sister, Samantha, but with Oregon's dark hair.

"I took too long," Oregon admitted. "For that I owe you both an apology, and I hope you'll forgive me. I just wanted to know for sure…"

She looked up, meeting his gaze. He saw tears gather in her eyes and escape down the slopes of her cheeks. "I messed up," she whispered.

"Yeah, you did." Lilly wasn't all about forgiveness at the moment. Duke knew she'd get past it. She was that kind of kid.

"Lilly, your mom wanted to know that I was a person she'd want in your life. And I can tell you, a few years back, I wasn't. I've made a lot of mistakes."

She shot him a look. "Yeah, you did."

"No. You're not a mistake," he countered.

"Not a mistake, just…" She grabbed her crutches and stood. "What am I?"

"Our daughter," Duke said, wishing he could take back twelve years and redo everything. But he couldn't.

"I'm taking a walk." Lilly hobbled off.

Duke started to go after her. Oregon stopped him, a hand on his arm. "Let her have a few minutes alone."

He sat back down in the chair next to Oregon. He watched his daughter walk away,

Daisy at her heels but keeping a careful distance. He knew where she was going. She was going to the horses.

"What are we going to do?" he asked Oregon. She was watching Lilly walk away.

"We're going to be parents together. We'll figure it out."

"Right. Of course we will." But Oregon had already figured it out. He was the one who had a lot to learn.

He'd spent most of his life not planning to marry, not planning on kids. And now he had one. A girl named Lilly. And where did that leave Oregon, the mother of his child?

Since yesterday he'd been forcing himself to remember, trying to recall that summer. Man, he'd been out of control that year. He'd watched his dad drinking his life away, Jake trying to be the man of the house and his younger siblings, Samantha and Brody, lost and alone. Duke had run wild, trying to make it all go away. But he remembered bits and pieces of a girl who thought she was having an adventure barrel racing.

Yeah, he remembered. She'd flirted, riding past him, taking his hat. He'd forgotten. He shouldn't have forgotten.

He looked at the woman sitting across from

him, worry over their daughter furrowing her brow. She was no longer that young girl. Duke saw her now as a mom, a woman with strength and faith.

And the mother of his child.

Chapter Four

Oregon started packing the next morning. By noon she had already made a dent in the process. Not that she had a lot. She'd always known how to let go of possessions, to keep only what really mattered.

An hour in, she'd sent Lilly across the street to talk to Duke. Since she'd been gone, Oregon had managed to go through twice as much, packing a lot and putting other things in boxes to be given away. She taped the top of a box she'd just filled and reached for another.

She hated moving. It brought back too many memories. Of leaving towns she would have liked to remain in and people she wanted to know better. By the time she'd reached her teens, she had stopped getting attached. It made it easier to let go if she shrugged it all off and pretended it didn't matter. A new home, a new life, a new opportunity, her mother had always said, as she had happily packed them off in some aging car she'd bought when the last aging car quit.

Oregon had moved here with the intention of putting down roots.

"Do you always talk to yourself?"

Oregon smiled at the woman standing outside the screen door of the apartment she and Lilly had called home since moving to Martin's Crossing. Apartment was a generous word for the small space, which was really just a living area with a bedroom in the loft.

"It stops me from saying things to the wrong people if I say them to myself." She motioned Breezy Martin in. "Want a cup of tea?"

"No, I'm good. I stopped by to see if I could help."

"I'm almost packed." She looked around her at the growing stacks of packed boxes. She didn't want to leave this cramped, tiny space that had been her home, a place where she and her daughter had been happy.

"I didn't mean help with packing." Breezy picked up a snow globe from the shelf and wrapped it in paper. "Although I will help pack. I meant, do you need a friend?"

Friends. Yes, she and Breezy had become friends since the other woman arrived in Martin's Crossing six months ago. And now Breezy would be Lilly's aunt. Because Breezy was married to Duke's brother, Jake Martin.

"Duke is in the clouds over this situation, Oregon," Breezy said.

Oregon held a carved horse in her hands and stared at the wall. She ached inside, wishing away this situation and how it was changing all of their lives. "I know he is."

"How is Lilly doing?"

Oregon shrugged and placed the horse in a box. "She's doing better physically. Getting used to the crutches and the fact that she won't spend her summer vacation swimming." She drew in a breath. "She's angry. At me. At Duke. At the world. But she's with him at the diner, because she's still trying to save up money for a horse, and he offered to let her work the cash register today."

"He wants to buy her a horse," Breezy offered. "He'd buy her the moon if he could."

"She doesn't need that. Buying her everything she wants won't solve the heartache."

"No, it won't." Breezy reached for another dust collector to wrap in paper.

"I have too many snow globes and knick-knacks." Oregon looked around the tiny living space. "Why do I collect things?"

Breezy smiled at that. "Now that is something I have an answer for. Because we moved so much as children. Things mean stability, having a home. If you collect something, you take it with you so that every new place feels a little familiar. Like home."

Oregon agreed as she looked at the shelves filled with things she'd collected. She had moved often as a girl because her mom couldn't stay in a relationship. Breezy, on the other hand, had spent much of her life drifting and homeless. Oregon wanted more for her daughter. She wanted a place where Lilly could have roots, family, a real home.

"I'm happy for my daughter. She loves Duke. She's loved him since the day we got to town. I just don't want him to let her down. I don't want to lose her, either."

"You won't lose her. And if ever there was a guy who wouldn't let a kid down, it's Duke Martin."

"In my heart I know that." But old hurts were hard to let go of. So many men had let her down. Starting with her own father, a man whose name she didn't even know, and ending with Duke, who should have remembered her. It was hard to put her trust in him now.

She taped the box and gave herself a lecture about trusting. Because she knew that she could trust God. She knew that He wouldn't let her down. He wouldn't go away. He wouldn't change His mind. Whatever happened with Duke, with Lilly, she knew they would get through this.

"I'm going to bring a casserole to the new place this evening so you don't have to worry about cooking." Breezy reached for an empty box.

"Thank you."

Breezy set the box down on the table and reached for a stack of books. "Why did you come here after so many years? I guess we all wondered what changed."

Fair questions. Duke had also asked, pushing to know more about her sudden appearance after so many years. He had wanted to know about the years in between, when she hadn't thought it was a good idea to tell him about Lilly.

Life changes and so do people, she had told him the previous day. But she hadn't told him that sometimes things happen and a mother realizes her little girl might someday need a safety net, another parent if one has to go away.

Her heart ached at the thought of ever having to leave her little girl alone. She wanted to be in her daughter's life for decades, not years. She wanted to watch Lilly grow up. See her get married, have children and grow older.

"Oregon, are you okay?"

She nodded, somehow looking at her friend with eyes free of tears. "Of course. I'm just emotional. I love this silly apartment."

Breezy shot her a look and shook her head. "I do not believe you are that attached to this place. And when you change your mind about talking, I'm here."

"I know you are." She managed to keep her hands from trembling. "What are people in town going to say? How will they treat her now that they know?"

Breezy put down the cup she'd been about to wrap and hugged Oregon tight. And Oregon didn't back away. She closed her eyes to fend off tears but held on to her friend.

"People love you, and they love your daughter. That isn't going to change."

"But life is going to change."

"Yeah, that's something we can't avoid." Breezy released her. Oregon listened to the brush of crutches on the sidewalk. Lilly was home.

Oregon hurried to open the door for her daughter, and Lilly gave her an "I can do it myself" look.

"Are you done working for the day?" Oregon asked as Lilly looked around the room at boxes nearly packed and empty walls and shelves.

Her daughter nodded. "I'm finished."

"Did you have fun?" Oregon winced at the question. Lilly shot her a look of disbelief.

"Of course I had fun. Just… I'm not sure what to call Duke. He used to be my friend. Now he's my dad."

Oregon didn't know how to respond, to the question or to the not-so-well-disguised anger. "Call him whatever feels right."

"Yeah, okay. Anyway, he said to tell you to come over and eat lunch."

"Thanks, honey."

Lilly shrugged and looked at the boxes, her back to Oregon and Breezy.

Oregon hadn't known what to expect when Lilly learned the truth about Duke. In her mind she'd played through several scenarios.

In one, Lilly had been thrilled, loving both of them, accepting that they would both love her, even if they couldn't be a family. In another, Lilly had rejected Duke and in the third, she had rejected Oregon.

They paled in comparison to the truth. The truth was a child who watched both parents, wary and unsure of the future. Reality was a flash of pain in blue eyes, accusing and angry.

Oregon had done this to her daughter. With her choices, first not to tell Duke and then to wait until now, when it felt too late.

Breezy slid a knowing gaze from Lilly to Oregon and offered a sympathetic look. "I should go. The twins are due for a nap, and Jake said something about cattle he has to work. Marty is off today."

The door closed softly behind her, followed by retreating steps. Oregon watched Lilly as she eased around boxes, her eyes focusing on trinkets that had been wrapped and packed to go.

"I'm sorry. I know I've said it before, but I'll say it again until you believe me. Or forgive me."

Lilly didn't look at her, but there was a shudder to her indrawn breath that hinted at tears. "I know. You were young and afraid.

Duke was no good. He wasn't responsible. He forgot you, and then he left."

Lilly's voice trembled as she repeated every word Oregon had said, tossing the words back at her, letting her hear the flimsiness of the explanations. She ached inside. She wanted to reach for her daughter but knew that Lilly would reject the comfort, and she didn't think she could handle the rejection right now.

"I made a lot of mistakes."

"Yeah, I know," Lilly said.

Oregon chilled on the inside. "No, you don't know. You weren't a mistake."

"No?"

"No, you weren't."

Lilly shrugged, and her eyes narrowed a bit. "But the Bible says…"

And there it was. How to tell a child she wasn't a mistake when the Bible clearly said it was. She'd given herself to a man who wasn't her husband. She'd had a child out of wedlock. The lesson had been taught at church, and Oregon had reinforced it at home. A young woman should cherish her purity.

"You weren't a mistake. I was young and unhappy, and I made a mistake. But I have never regretted having you. You kept me sane. You kept me focused. I'm not sure where I would be without you, Lilly. I think I'd be lost. Physically and spiritually, probably emotionally. So you were not a mistake. I'm not sure how to connect something I did that I shouldn't have and the gift you have been, but God is merciful, and somehow He knew that through my mistake something beautiful would happen."

Lilly edged around her to the door. "We should go."

Oregon closed her eyes, fighting tears that stung and the tight ache in her throat. "I love you."

"Mom, I know you love me. And I love you. But I'm still mad."

Oregon sobbed, the tears rolling down her cheeks. She closed the distance between herself and Lilly, wrapping the girl in the embrace they both needed. Lilly tried to break away, but Oregon held her tight.

"Please, forgive me."

"I forgive you, Mom."

But the tense set of young shoulders told Oregon more than words. She was forgiven, but the anger wasn't going away. Not today.

From the kitchen of Duke's No Bar and Grill, Duke heard Oregon's voice, soft and vulnerable. He stirred the big pot of spaghetti sauce that would be the evening special, then headed for the dining room of the restaurant. He'd owned Duke's for a couple of years. He had needed this place when he first got back from Afghanistan. Cooking had given him a way to focus on something other than the pain of memories.

Ned, short for Nedine, had seated Lilly and Oregon at a booth by the window. He smiled at the waitress, a big woman with a heart of gold. She winked as she walked past him. He thought she had probably guessed the situation with himself, Oregon and Lilly. He hadn't really made it public knowledge, but nothing got past Ned.

His brothers knew. Jake and Brody were both supportive. Jake in his typical older-brother, serious and a little self-righteous way. Brody had halfheartedly teased. But Brody hadn't been the same since he came back to Martin's Crossing, saying he was done with riding bulls and with his best friend and traveling buddy. Something had shifted in their little brother. He was a little bit angry and too determined to find the mother who had walked out on them twenty years ago.

Duke hadn't yet got around to telling Samantha, their little sister, about Lilly. She was in college and doing better than she had been a few years ago. She'd finally forgiven them for sending her away. Maybe she was actually starting to see that they'd done her a favor.

As he walked toward the booth, Lilly looked up at him, her blue eyes issuing a challenge. Claim me or else, those eyes said. He had no problem claiming her. What he wanted more than anything was to wipe away the anger and hurt. From her expression and from Oregon's. How did he do that?

How did he go from bachelor to father? With only twenty-four hours behind them, he was still struggling with that. His first instinct was to give his kid a pony. Oregon had made it clear Lilly had to earn the money. Instead, he'd given them a house to live in.

He needed to make them a family. It wasn't a comfortable thought. He hadn't ever imagined himself married. Not even close. He definitely hadn't imagined kids. He loved his twin nieces, Violet and Rose, but he hadn't imagined having any of his own. For a lot of reasons. How would he know how to be a dad when his own parents had checked out? Why would he want to give up a pretty easy life as a bachelor?

He now had an answer to that last question. When a man faced a kid like Lilly, it became easy to think of giving up the single life.

"How about some lunch?" he offered, because it seemed to him that Oregon would be more likely to take lunch from him than a marriage proposal. What had he been thinking, proposing to her in a hospital hallway? He might be a bachelor, but he did know a thing or two about romance.

"Cheeseburger and fries, and a strawberry shake." Lilly ordered with the slightest hint of a smile.

Oregon stared at the menu blankly.

Duke grabbed a chair from a nearby table, turned it backward and sat with his arms rested on the chair back. Oregon glanced his way, her gray eyes wary. She refocused on the menu she still held in hands that trembled just the slightest bit. He waited, giving her time. He knew this game. It was like breaking a horse. Slow and gentle, giving them time to trust, to accept.

Trust. He had a feeling neither of them were really big on trusting. He'd watched her for the past year, easing into the community, keeping to herself for the most part, then eventually letting a few people in.

He'd been abandoned by his own mother. He understood what it meant to have trust issues. He also knew he couldn't fix everything. As a medic in the army, he'd tried. And he'd walked away, disillusioned with his own abilities and with God, because he knew God had to hear him screaming for help saving those kids.

He cleared his throat, coming back to the present, away from dark memories that he usually kept at bay until night. Oregon watched him closely with eyes that seemed to see too much.

"So what about you?" he asked as he studied her face. He shifted his gaze to Lilly. Not for the first time he wondered how he'd been so blind. Breezy had told him she noticed the first time she met Lilly. Jake had nodded, as if everyone had seen the resemblance.

"I'll take a chef salad," Oregon answered.

He started to stand but Ned was there, round face smiling big and her graying auburn hair in a long ponytail. Nedine, fifty and happily single, was half hippy and half rancher, and when she settled her hand on his shoulder, he didn't argue. He stayed put.

"I've got this, boss." She winked and held

up her order pad. "How about I fix you some lunch and you can join the ladies?"

"I'll take the same as Lilly. And thank you."

She winked and walked away. He stood, moving his chair back to the neighboring table. Lilly scooted, making room for him in the booth. He slid in next to her, their shoulders bumping. He looked down, and she looked up at him, her teeth biting into her bottom lip as she studied his face.

Was she seeing the resemblance? he wondered. He guessed she was because she frowned, first at him and then at her mom.

Oregon's cheeks turned pink, and she focused on the napkin in her hands. He had to get control of the situation. That was the first step in this new life of his. Staying in control.

"I've got Ned and Joe working tonight." At the mention of Joe, Oregon looked up. Suspicion settled in her eyes, because that's the reaction everyone in town had to the drifter who had shown up before Christmas.

Oregon thanked Ned, who set a glass of sweet tea in front of her and the shakes in front of Lilly and himself. The waitress scurried away, fast for a woman so large.

"I thought I'd take the night off and help you move."

"Oh, I see."

Did she have another plan? Someone else who would help?

"Is that okay?" He leaned forward, folding his large frame a little so that he didn't tower over Oregon and his daughter. Even sitting, he knew he towered. A man who was six foot eight knew he could be intimidating.

"Yes, of course," Lilly answered, sounding way too grown-up. That gave him pause. She was twelve, but she would soon grow up.

He got a little itchy thinking about that. She'd be a teenager. She'd date. There would be boys knocking on the door, and she would get in a car and go out with them. He swallowed a lump of fear that got tangled up with premature anger. If the boys were anything like him, they weren't coming near Lilly.

A foot connected with his shin, and he managed not to squawk at the sharp pain. He glanced at the woman sitting across from him as she gave him a warning look.

"What?" he fairly snarled.

"That's my cue to take a walk." Lilly pushed his shoulder. "Grown-up talk time. And I don't even know why. I get a family and suddenly we can't sit down to a meal without the adults acting like they're at war."

He moved from the booth and watched as she situated her crutches and scurried away. She glanced back over her shoulder. "I'm going to the kitchen. Let me know when you're done talking about me."

Duke folded himself back into the booth and felt like a ten-year-old kid that had been sent to the principal's office. He glanced at the woman sitting across from him. She didn't openly smile, but he saw her lips start to curve, the flicker of amusement in her eyes.

"Did we say something that made her think we needed time to talk?" he asked.

Her grin became the real deal. He loved that gesture, the way it shifted her face, and the sweetness settled in her eyes. That smile made him regret the past, making him not so sorry about the present or the future. But nervous. Yeah, still nervous.

"You looked like a thundercloud," Oregon responded, and he blinked.

"What does that mean?"

"You were sitting there all calm and gentle giant-like, and suddenly you became a rumbling mountain about to erupt."

"I didn't realize."

"No, I'm sure you didn't. You rumble. It almost sounds like a growl. And I'm sure Lilly is wondering why."

He leaned back in the seat, the vinyl cushion lumpy from overuse, ripped a bit in one spot. He'd have to fix that. Oregon kicked him again, this time without the power of that first time. He opened his eyes and looked at her.

"I was thinking about the fact that I just got this kid, and in the next few years she's going to become a young lady," he admitted, feeling all kinds of insecurity that a grown man shouldn't feel. "And she'll, well, she'll date. Boys. I'll have to hurt them."

Oregon laughed, the sound so easy and warm that it slid over him like summer rain. He soaked it up, like a man dying of thirst who hadn't even known he was thirsty.

"Yes, she'll date. And you won't hurt them."

"What if she brings home a guy like me, the way I was at sixteen or seventeen?" He grimaced at none-too-pleasant memories. "At twenty."

"She's not me, and she isn't going to date anyone like you. She is loved and secure, and I hope she'll make better choices. And I'm not going to let her randomly date every boy that knocks on the door or calls. Or texts."

"Gotcha. But I can be there."

"And intimidate them?"

She glanced at his interlocked fingers, and he made an effort to relax his hands.

"Never." He grinned as he said it. Something inside him loosened a bit. At least Oregon had time on the job, as a parent, as a mom.

He wondered if she would resent his participation. Maybe now was the time to talk. They hadn't talked much since he'd taken them home yesterday. No, yesterday had been more about telling Lilly, and then watching her shut down and wondering how to fix everything.

"I want to be a part of her life, Oregon. I want to be more than the neighbor, the guy who watches her grow up. I want to be a father to her."

"I assumed you would." Her voice was easy, only a hint of tension. "That's why I came here, Duke. I know I should have told you sooner, but it wasn't that easy. Once I got here, I realized that bringing you into her life meant bringing you into mine. It just wasn't as simple as I had convinced myself it would be."

"Eventually we have to talk about why you made the decision now, after twelve years of parenting alone." Because he knew there had been something that pushed her to come here, something to change her mind.

"It's a long story."

"That's just your way of saying *none of your business*, right?"

"No, not really. It's just a long story."

There were tears building in her eyes, hanging on her lashes. The door to the kitchen opened. That would be their lunch. It would also mean the return of Lilly. He let it go. For now.

He also let go of the very real urge to hug the woman sitting across from him.

Chapter Five

The truck and trailer pulling up to Oregon's apartment later that afternoon took her by surprise. She watched as Duke's brothers, Jake and Brody, jumped down from the truck. Brody hopped a little on one leg, shook his right leg out and then pretended that at twenty-six there wasn't a thing wrong with him. He wasn't as tall as his older brothers. He was more lean than muscular. His dark hair was a little too long, and his blue eyes hinted at something going on that he kept hidden deep down where no one would care to try to excavate it.

Jake, on the other hand, looked like the happy newlywed he was. He'd married Breezy Hernandez just weeks ago and still had the look of a man who had found what he wanted when he hadn't even been looking. He waved as he pulled a handcart from the back of the truck.

"Someone called for Martin Moving, Inc?" he called out as he headed up the sidewalk.

Oregon held the door open, and from behind Lilly pushed her, wanting to see. "We don't have a lot."

"Then it won't take long," Brody supplied as he half limped up the sidewalk. "You just tell us what to do, and we'll do it." He stepped through the door, giving Lilly a playful nudge as he did. "Duke should be here soon. He had to make sure everything was taken care of for the dinner crowd."

"He'll try to find a way out of this," Jake informed her. "He hates moving."

"Talking about me, big brother?" Duke appeared in the doorway, a little taller than Jake and quite a bit wider in the shoulders. He might be younger by a few years, but Duke was no one's little brother.

Jake grinned as he started to stack boxes. "I'd never talk about you. Not much."

Oregon looked over at her daughter. Lilly watched in wide-eyed fascination as the brothers argued back and forth. She'd never been a part of a family, not one like this. They'd only had Oregon's mom and her newest husband until he became the ex-husband. They didn't have siblings, aunts, uncles, cousins.

By coming here, Oregon had given Lilly a family. She'd given her daughter a safety net, people to be there for her. It felt good. She felt secure in the knowledge that if something happened to her, Lilly would have the Martins.

"Hey, do you have tape?" Duke nudged her a little.

She shook her head. "Sorry. What?"

"You didn't hear a thing I said, did you?" he asked.

"No," she admitted. "Not sure where I was."

"Far away." He smiled as he said it, that smile indicating that maybe they would be friends. Friendship would make things easier between them, easier for Lilly. Friendship meant someone having her back.

She drifted back to reality. "So…tape?"

He arched a brow. "Yes, tape."

She went to get it. When she returned, Lilly was sitting next to Brody, telling him about the last place they'd lived in and how she'd spent time with a friend of her mom's for a month. Brody looked up and saw her watching them. He winked and went back to work, still listening to Lilly's stories about Mississippi, Alabama and a small town in Oklahoma. For a time they'd tried to stay close to Oregon's mom, but that had proved exhausting. Oregon wanted stability for her daughter, not for her to be another victim of her mother's unsettled lifestyle.

"Do you want us to move this furniture into storage?" Duke asked as he headed for the door with boxes.

She shook her head. "No, I'll leave it here. When I'm in the shop, it's nice to have a place where Lilly can hang out."

"Works for me." Duke shouldered the door open and headed down the sidewalk.

Oregon grabbed two boxes and followed him. She wasn't sure why or what she planned on saying. As the door closed behind her, she heard Lilly call Duke's brother Uncle Brody.

Her heart tightened at the words. She hurried on, catching up with Duke.

"Following me?" Duke asked without looking back.

"I'm carrying boxes."

"Right." He shifted the boxes he carried and glanced at her, slowing just a little. "You have to stop worrying."

"I'm not worrying, I'm…"

"Worrying." He set the boxes in the back of the truck and then jumped up inside. "We'll get through this."

"I know we will."

She watched him stack boxes along the back of the truck. He turned, keeping his head low because the truck didn't allow for his height. "You don't sound convinced."

"I'm trying," she assured him.

He jumped down, landing next to her. He touched her cheek with a large, calloused hand, gently forcing her to look at him. Look into blue eyes that were as clear as a summer sky. His mouth curved in an easy smile as he leaned a little toward her. She focused on the dimples that appeared in his cheeks, because she could lose herself in his eyes, in the promises she saw in them.

"You need to start believing," he whispered. "Because I won't let us fail as a family."

Family. But they weren't a family, she thought to tell him, but she couldn't form the words. For a moment she was lost because she'd honestly thought he meant to kiss her when he leaned close. And she couldn't let that happen. Could she?

The idea of kissing him seemed almost as dangerous as the idea of believing the three of them would be a real family. That wasn't why she'd come here. She'd come to Martin's Crossing to give Lilly a chance at being a part of a family, but she hadn't included herself in that plan.

She looked up at Duke, putting a stop to the moment stretching between them. "Of course you won't let us fail. We're in this together. We'll be fine."

They were in a mess, is what they were in. He knew how it felt to have a family fall apart. She knew how it felt to never have a father. She also knew that if he kissed her she would fall for him all over again. And she couldn't do that.

Because she knew how it felt to be walked out on. Not once, or even twice, but over and over again. Whatever the cost, she would protect her heart. She would protect her daughter.

"I know we'll be fine," she repeated, ignoring his amused look.

"Of course we will. And you've got to learn to relax."

"I know how to relax."

He winked, which didn't help matters at all. Maybe she shouldn't have worried about the influence he would have on her daughter. Maybe her first concern should be for how he could undo all of her very carefully groomed self-preservation.

"Here comes Joe and Mr. Mueller. Two of your biggest fans. And maybe I shouldn't feel so relaxed because they're puffed up like bodyguards."

"As if those two could hurt you."

He grinned at that. "Of course they could."

"Oregon, I hear you're leaving the neighborhood," Mr. Mueller, dapper with thinning gray hair, asked as he stepped close to her.

He was the grandson of German immigrants and owned a small store next to Oregon's where he sold the wood carvings and candle carousel nativities that his grandfather had first made in Germany. A skill that had been passed down through generations, he explained to those who shopped in his store.

"We're not leaving, Mr. Mueller, just relocating temporarily. And of course I'll still be at the shop."

"Of course she will," Joe added. "We wouldn't let Oregon leave us for good."

Joe had been so kind since his arrival in town. He'd often stopped by to help her take out trash or carry shipments to the post office. He'd helped Lilly find homes for the puppies their dog had given birth to last winter. She really liked Joe, but she was still wary.

"No, we aren't going anywhere," she confirmed.

Joe glanced past her, his eyes lighting, and she knew that the beaming look was for Lilly. She heard the brush of the crutches on the sidewalk, and she turned to watch her daughter make steady progress toward them. Her pace almost a little too quick for a mother's peace of mind. Lilly grinned at her, as if she knew Oregon's thoughts.

"Brody and Jake are bringing out a bunch of boxes, and they said Duke might want to get back in there and help. Instead of socializing," Lilly said in a slightly deeper tone, to emulate the men inside.

Duke saluted, chuckling as he headed inside. Oregon knew that he felt every bit the proud father, as if he'd just seen a newborn for the first time. But his daughter was long past infancy, past first words and first steps. She was a walking, talking—and very rotten— twelve-year-old, who would keep her daddy wrapped around her little finger.

Oregon sighed. She knew she had to work overtime to keep her daughter on firm footing.

And to keep Duke from giving her everything she'd always wanted.

Duke carried the last load of boxes from the truck to the cottage where Oregon was already putting things away, turning what had been his home into hers. He walked through the back door and noticed her dark hair was pulled back in a ponytail as she swiped at perspiration on her brow. He guessed she was worn out, physically and emotionally. The last few days hadn't been easy on any of them.

"This is the last of it. Jake and Brody left, and I think we should take a break." Duke placed the boxes on the kitchen floor and moved next to the woman standing at the sink, her back to him.

"A break would be good. But you don't have to stay. We'll probably eat sandwiches and go to bed early."

"Are you saying you want me to go?" He waited, not pushing. She turned on the water and ran her hands under it for a few seconds, splashed her face, then reached for a paper towel. "Oregon, it's going to work out."

"I know it is." She tossed the paper towel in the trash and looked around, as if seeing the kitchen for the first time. "This is perfect, really. You can spend time with Lilly. We're in the country, and her dog is obviously much happier. Everything is perfect."

Then she started to cry.

What did he do with a woman standing in his kitchen, falling apart in front of him?

He took a chance and wrapped his arms around her, pulling her close. She didn't object; instead she leaned into his shoulder and sobbed against him. He kept her close, brushing a hand down her back, rubbing until the sobs lessened.

"We're going to make it through this, Oregon. We're going to give our girl what she needs to be happy. She's going to have us both."

She nodded, but he could tell from the damp warmth seeping into his T-shirt that she continued to cry.

Then the back door slammed. Followed by a startled "Oops."

He smiled back at Lilly as she raised a crutch to wave, and then she backed out the door again. Her dog and his went with her. He watched from the window as she settled on the bench glider in the yard. Her dog, Belle, climbed up next to her, stretched out and rested her head on Lilly's lap.

"I have to stop being so emotional." Oregon finally sniffled and stepped away from him. She reached for another paper towel. "I didn't come to town for myself. I came here for Lilly."

"Right, of course. And just so you know, it isn't wrong for you to need someone. And I think you've done a lot of that in your life, with no one ever there to help."

"I'm good at taking care of myself."

"Yeah, I know. But let me be here for you. And for Lilly. Stop worrying that I'm going to take her away from you."

"But you could."

"I think you know better. The two of you are a team. If anyone should be jealous, it should be me."

"So now we'll be a team of three."

He hugged her once more, because yes, that's exactly what they would be. A team of three. He'd be living at his place, even as he finished the renovations. They'd be here in the cottage. It wasn't perfect, but for now it was a place to start.

"Do you need me to do anything else before I leave for the night?"

"Have a sandwich with us. Breezy's casserole was good, but I'm starving again."

"Sit outside with Lilly, and I'll bring everything out."

Her hand rested on his arm, just briefly. "I can make my own sandwich."

"I know you can, but humor me. Go have a seat. The sun is down, and it's pretty nice out there. You can't always grab a cool night like this in Texas, so take advantage of it."

She started to argue, but he pushed her out the back door, gentle hands on her shoulders. He watched as she walked across the patio. Lilly met her at the table. Belle, the Border collie he'd given Lilly when she first moved to town and seemed to need a friend, followed. The dog curled at Lilly's feet when she sat in the chair next to her mother.

Not much scared Duke. But this scared him senseless. These two people were counting on him. They were counting on him to be there for them, to provide, to stay sober.

He hadn't thought much about staying sober for the past year or so. There had been a time when every day sobriety was a struggle. Every day sober had been a victory. He'd had to accept that the bottle had been his hiding place. The place he'd run to when he couldn't handle pain or anger. He wouldn't run back to that bottle again.

He walked out the back door carrying a tray with bottles of water, sandwiches and a bag of chips. Oregon jumped up to help. She had kicked off her shoes, and she looked young and even a little bit carefree in cut-off jean shorts and a T-shirt, her dark hair pulled back off her face.

But carefree stopped at her eyes. Those eyes reflected her every mood and pulled him in, making him want to know more about her thoughts. He shook it off.

"Let me help."

He slid the tray onto the table. "I think I've got it covered. I do own a diner, you know."

Lilly reached for a sandwich almost immediately. He grinned at the kid and put a bottle of water in front of her. She grinned back at him. Kids. They bounced back quickly. But it mattered more than ever that she be happy, that she relax and not worry.

He took the chair next to hers. He'd never liked this patio furniture. It felt like a miniature set, not a set built for a man his size.

"Are you going to church with us tomorrow?" Lilly asked as she bit into the ham sandwich.

Oregon shot her a warning look. He didn't know if she was warning her not to talk with her mouth full or if it was about church. Yeah, everyone in town knew that he hadn't gone to church much since he got back from Afghanistan. He was sure there were a few prayer chains with his name on them.

"I'm not sure about that, but I'll cook burgers on the grill when you get home," he offered, hoping it would get him off the hook.

Lilly just shrugged and looked a little down. He drew in a breath and tried to find another reasonable excuse. Oregon ate her sandwich silently, ignoring his predicament. Of course she did.

"You put her up to this?" When they both erupted in big grins, he finally caught on.

Oregon looked up, all innocent and beautiful in the moonlight that cast a silvery beam across the lawn. "Never."

He shook his head and finished a second sandwich. "Right."

"We could all go together," Lilly suggested, as if that made it easier.

Oregon shook her head. "Lilly, enough."

His daughter shot him a look, then she stood, adjusting crutches under her arms. "Okay, then. I'm going to bed. It's been a long day."

He watched her go, thinking she was

probably giving them time alone. She was a smart kid.

"I'm sorry for letting her back you into a corner."

"Don't worry about it." He leaned back in the chair. "But I can't do it, Oregon. Not yet. There are a lot of reasons why."

"Care to talk about it?" Her tone was soft, and yeah, he would like to talk about it. Someday.

"Not tonight. I think I should go."

She walked him to his truck, and for a long time they stood there, the moon almost full above them. He had a lot to say. From the way she was studying everything but him, he guessed she felt the same.

Sometimes words just got in the way of what a person really wanted. And at that moment the one thing Duke wanted was Oregon Jeffries in his arms. Even if she said no, even if he would regret it tomorrow, he was willing to take the chance.

He took a step toward her. As he placed a hand on her back and pulled her a little closer, she looked up at him as if she didn't have a clue what he was about to do. He leaned in, and her eyes widened. Yeah, she wasn't clueless any longer.

The first brush of his lips against hers settled it in his mind. He wanted Oregon. He wanted her in his arms, in his life. She started to pull away, but as his mouth claimed hers, she slowly kissed him back, her hands touching his arms, resting lightly on his skin. When his lips left hers and settled near her temple, he heard her soft sigh.

He didn't know if he could ever pull away from this woman. Physically maybe, but emotionally, he wasn't sure. Because in his arms, she felt right. In his arms, everything felt right. It had been a long time since he could say that about his life.

Eventually she stepped out of his arms. The last thing he wanted to see in her expression, in her eyes, was regret. But there it was, and it sliced right through him. Of course she would regret this. Of course she would think he was the same man who had used her and walked away thirteen years ago.

He drew her back and held her for a minute. "You feel good in my arms, Oregon. This feels right."

She gave a quick shake of her head. "No. This will just be a complication. Please, just be here for Lilly."

The last words didn't make sense. "Of course I'm going to be here for Lilly."

Did she doubt him?

"Promise me, Duke. That's what I need from you."

"Promises can be broken, Oregon. But I'm telling you that I'll always be in my daughter's life."

"Thank you." She stood on tiptoe and kissed his cheek.

Then she walked away. He stood there, watching as she went up the walk to the front door. She paused, framed in the porch light, to wave goodbye before going inside.

As he drove home he tried to make sense of what she'd said. He understood that she'd doubt him. Sometimes he doubted himself. But what Oregon had said sounded as if it was more about her and less about him.

Whatever it was, he would figure it out.

Chapter Six

The sun hadn't topped the eastern horizon when Oregon heard a loud banging from the direction of the barn the next morning. She started a pot of coffee and headed out the back door. The sky was still gray and the grass damp with dew that soaked through her canvas shoes. In the fog-shrouded field, the horses grazed, obviously not caring about the noise.

The steady banging sound started again. She walked through the front door of the old barn, inhaling the scent of livestock and hay. The racket continued, reverberating in the stillness of early morning. She made her way to the double doors on the opposite end of the building, pushing them open slowly. Daylight seeped in, chasing away the shadows.

She walked through the back doors and into

a mess. Duke was hammering on an old tractor, his shirt already drenched in sweat, his biceps bulging as he pounded. After another strike or two on the rusted metal, he tossed the mallet or whatever he'd been using. Oregon jumped back, and it landed just a few feet from where she'd been standing.

"You okay?" She took tentative steps in his direction.

He swiped his arm across his brow. He didn't smile. No customary Duke grin or even a wink to show that he wasn't worked up about something.

"I'm fine."

"Is this about learning you have a daughter?"

He walked past her to pick up the mallet. "No, of course not."

"Any way I can help?"

"No, there's no way you can help." And then he swiped a hand across his face. "I didn't mean to wake you up. I'm used to being alone out here."

Friendship would make things easier between them. Or would that lead to complications she didn't want? "Being alone is good sometimes, but there are times when it helps to talk with a friend."

"I appreciate it, Oregon. But I'm good. I'm just chasing away some memories."

"I know." Her heart ached for him, for what he was hiding so deep down that it woke him before dawn each morning.

"I'm going to church with you today. I should go. Lilly wants me to go."

"She'll understand if you don't want—"

He raised a hand to cut her off. "Don't. I know she'll understand. But I'm not going to be that guy, the one who isn't there for his kid. She wants me to go to church, and I'm not so selfish that I'm going to ignore that just to nurse my own anger."

"Are you angry?"

"Oregon, are you ready to tell me why you suddenly decided to make an entrance in my life with my daughter?"

"There isn't anything to tell."

"I don't buy that."

She looked away, toward the sun that touched the morning with golden light that would soon dissipate the fog, the dew, the coolness in the air. "I have coffee on."

"Now that's an offer I'll take."

"And if you ever want to talk…" Did she really want to talk with him, to share their stories? It felt safer to place him in neat little boxes. Lilly's dad. Owner of Duke's. Brother of Jake. Anything else and she was adding layers. Layers that would show his humanity.

She kept telling herself that the only thing she wanted from Duke was a man who wouldn't walk out on her daughter. It was easier that way. It kept her heart safe. No one walked out on her if she didn't let them into her life in the first place.

"I hope it's plain coffee," Duke said.

"Plain?"

"I'm not a fan of flavored beans. Give me good old-fashioned coffee, and I'm happy."

"No whipped cream, no ice, no mocha?" she teased, and her mood lightened, like the sky. Blue was chasing the gray away, leaving a clear sky, a beautiful morning.

"Just good, black coffee."

She opened her back door and motioned him inside. "You're in luck. I'm a fan of plain old coffee, too."

They were sitting on the patio when Lilly hopped out the back door, spotted them, made a face and then joined them at the table. "What's for breakfast?"

"Cereal." Oregon stood, and then she looked at Duke. "Do you want a bowl or just coffee?"

"Just coffee," he answered. As Oregon

walked away she heard their conversation turn to horses. Lilly was still upset that her summer would be spent on crutches and not in the saddle the way she'd planned. Duke told her there were things she could do. And then he was telling her about a nice gelding he'd recently bought.

Oregon felt control slipping away.

Her phone rang as she poured milk on cereal. She reached for it as she emptied the coffeepot into a thermos. "Hi, Mom."

"Honey, how is my granddaughter doing?" Eugenia Barker sounded sweet and homey over the phone, like any grandmother might. She sounded like a woman who baked cookies and made casseroles. But she wasn't that woman, had never been that woman.

She randomly jumped from one fad diet to the next. The latest was the "only fruits and vegetables that had dropped from the plant" diet. In Oregon's opinion, it seemed extreme. Not that she had anything against vegans or vegetarians, she just didn't like her mother's extravagances. Including her newest get-rich-quick scheme, some antiaging product she was selling out of her trunk as she traveled across the country. Eugenia knew how to reinvent herself.

"Lilly is fine. She's in less pain and getting used to the crutches," Oregon answered as she continued to peer out the window.

"I'm so glad. I thought I'd stop in next week and see the two of you."

"Oh." What else could she say? It would be rude to tell her not to visit. But it was tempting. After all, her last visit to town had included attempting to halt an Easter concert in the park. Oregon wasn't sure if her mother really opposed a Christian concert or if she just got a kick from causing problems.

"You don't want me to visit? I thought you were all about forgiveness. The concert debacle was a year ago."

"I know it was, Mom. And I do forgive." It was the lifetime of instability that she had a hard time letting go of. It was the half-dozen stepfathers, all of whom she was required to call Daddy. It was the blank her mother had left on her birth certificate and Eugenia's refusal to reveal her father's identity.

"Of course you do. And I know Lilly will love what I'm bringing her."

"Mom, what are you bringing?"

"Oh, don't get all upset. It's small and won't cause you any trouble."

"Don't."

"I'm your mother. I get to decide what I will and won't do."

Right, of course. That's the way Oregon had lived her life—at her mother's whim. The moves, the new husbands, the new religions and diets, it had all been up to her mother. Oregon had been dragged along like a puppy on a leash.

"I'll be there in a few days," Eugenia said. "Gotta go, sweetie. I've got an appointment."

"Sure. Have a wonderful Sunday, Mom."

"You know I will. I have vitamins to deliver."

Oregon groaned as she ended the call. The last thing she wanted or needed was her mother invading. The back door opened. Duke ducked his head as he stepped inside. He gave her a cautious look.

"I thought I should see if the cereal is still crunchy and the coffee still hot. And Lilly said, from the bits of conversation that we heard, that it must be her grandmother calling to brighten your day."

"Yes, Eugenia Barker will be here sometime next week."

"Well, good. Martin's Crossing has gotten a little boring." He grinned as he said it, picking up the thermos and two cups.

"I like boring," she said. "Boring is calm. It doesn't take a person by surprise. Boring doesn't include my mother, which makes it more attractive."

"Boring isn't a challenge," he teased. "You bring the cereal bowls."

"I'm going to pour them out and start over."

"Starting over isn't always such a bad idea," Duke said as he walked away.

Oregon closed her eyes and stood for a long moment, thinking about what he'd said. She could attach so many meanings to his one sentence. Starting over with him. Starting over on her relationship with her mother.

Starting over in Martin's Crossing.

Duke had avoided church for a long time. He'd avoided God and the thoughts of God that plagued him at night. He'd avoided prayer. Not because he didn't believe, but because he couldn't get past his anger. He had a long list of unanswered prayers. The list started with the ones he'd said years ago, for a mom who'd left and never came back. For a dad who had given up. Most recently, prayers for men who had died in Afghanistan even though he'd desperately tried to save them.

It didn't seem fair that on this Sunday in

late May the sermon was about prayer. "The prayer of the righteous man availeth much," Pastor Allen repeated twice. What did that mean? That he wasn't righteous? That his prayers didn't count?

He wanted to get up from the pew and walk out, but Lilly sat on one side of him, and Oregon on the other. Jason Allen looked at him, as if he knew all the turmoil this sermon caused him. And Oregon seemed to know, too. Her hand reached for his, and she gave it a quick, reassuring squeeze.

Not too many people got it. They wanted him to get past it, to let it go. But he couldn't close his eyes without seeing faces. So many faces. And he remembered all the letters from home, from wives, from moms and dads, from children. He remembered all the pictures that those guys had shared with him.

"Sometimes we feel like our prayers are going unanswered, as if we're hitting our heads against a wall." Pastor Allen's words broke through the fog. Duke's gaze connected with his pastor's.

It was as if this sermon had been on hold, just waiting for his reappearance.

"Trust begins with accepting that God's got this, no matter what *this* is. God's got it. To be effective in prayer and to understand what we call 'unanswered prayers,' we have to comprehend that we see in bits and pieces, but God sees everything."

Duke got up and walked out. He didn't apologize. He didn't stop when Oregon tried to stop him. He left with all of his anger, all of his resentment, building like an inferno. Because words were easy when a person lived in Martin's Crossing, but men dying in battle, that was a whole other matter.

She caught up with him at his truck. He was shaking as he reached for the door, and her hand settled over his, stopping him. He started to tell her to go away, but he couldn't get the words out. He felt like he was about to cry, and he sure didn't want her to see that. A week ago she'd just been the pretty mom who lived and worked across the street from the diner. Today she was the mother of his daughter, and she was digging in deep where no one else dared to go.

Without saying a word she took his keys and told him to scoot to the passenger side. She climbed behind the wheel of his Ford King Ranch and started the thing, shifting into reverse, grinding the clutch enough to make him shudder. When the truck lurched forward a few times, it made him smile. He brushed at his eyes and leaned back in the seat, trying to let go of his anger, one sharp breath at a time.

"Lilly?" he finally asked as they were heading down the road.

"With Breezy."

She kept driving. He kept breathing, pushing past the sound of helicopters in his memory, of men, some just kids, crying out in pain. He'd held bandages on gaping wounds that wouldn't stop bleeding and tried his best to hold their hands as they faced eternity.

He'd prayed. He hadn't thought of himself as a righteous man, just one who wanted to save a life. He'd prayed, yelling at God to help him help those men.

Oregon parked his truck at the edge of the lake. And still she didn't say anything. No one else knew, the way she seemed to know, that he needed silence to process his thoughts, his pain.

"Want to walk with me?" he asked as he got out of the truck.

"Of course."

She met him at the water's edge, stepping carefully over the rocky ground. The water lapped the shore, and in the distance a boat motor broke the early-afternoon silence. Her hand reached for his, and he took it, holding tight as they walked.

"That was either the worst sermon to hear, or the best," he said as they came to a fishing dock. He led her onto the floating deck that rocked gently with waves caused by a ski boat.

"Both?" she offered as they sat on a bench.

"Yeah, both." He let out a sigh as his chest let go of the pressure that had been building over the past hour. "I can't forget their faces."

"I'm sorry." She didn't say more. He didn't want more. He didn't need to hear that someday he would forget, or that it would get easier. Maybe he didn't want either of those things to happen. Those soldiers who died didn't need to be forgotten. His life shouldn't get easier.

The woman sitting next to him gave a quiet, calm assurance with her very presence. He hadn't had a lot of calm in his life the past few years. He'd been happy. He'd kept busy. But calm? Not so much. He hadn't thought too much about it until lately, when she was at his side.

"I don't want to think about how God was okay with all those men dying," he admitted.

"I know. I don't blame you."

"Would you stop being so easy to get along

with?" He lifted her hand to his lips and held it there as he closed his eyes, thinking about how guilty he felt when he slept through the night without nightmares.

"One of us has to be easy to get along with," she said.

"Right."

He pulled her close to his side and held her, just held her.

"I don't think God was okay with those guys dying," she whispered against his shoulder. "I think He isn't okay with the pain it causes you. But I also think that those men were blessed to have you there with them."

The words poured over him like a balm, simple truths that were exactly what he'd needed someone to say. He held her a little tighter and realized he could get used to having this woman in his life.

It was something he'd never imagined, a woman in his life, a child that looked like him.

They were dangerous thoughts.

Chapter Seven

They sat together for a while on the dock, until a family spilled out of a van and headed down the ramp with coolers and fishing poles.

"Jake decided to take over cooking duty today," Duke said as he stood, reaching for her hand. "Burgers on the grill. If we go back now, we'll be in time for lunch and miss out on the work."

"Sounds like a plan." Oregon tossed him his keys. "I can't take you white-knuckling the door handle all the way home, so you'd better drive."

"You saw that?" He grinned, and she felt her heart shudder, half apprehension and half something else she didn't want to acknowledge.

"I saw it." She let him open the passenger door for her. "I didn't do that bad."

"Yeah, you did."

As he drove she pretended it was just another Sunday, and that they weren't heading for danger. After all, he was just supposed to be Lilly's safety net. He wasn't meant to be Oregon's. She definitely wasn't meant to be his. But she'd crossed a line, following him out of the church.

She just hadn't been able to let him leave alone. Not with that tortured look in his eyes.

"I wasn't going to fall apart," he said as they got close to the Circle M.

She glanced his way, surprised by the abrupt comment and the defensive tone.

"I know you weren't."

He didn't look at her, continuing to watch the road, his jaw tightening a little. Unsure wasn't something Duke Martin was used to feeling. He probably faced every situation with a certain amount of courage and certainty because of his size and his overwhelming confidence. Sometimes known as ego. She laughed to herself at the thought.

"I heard that."

She stared at the passing scenery. "I didn't say anything."

"You laughed."

"I chuckled. There's a difference. And I

wasn't laughing at you. Maybe at your ego, but not at you."

"Thanks. That's great for my self-esteem."

"You don't have a self-esteem issue."

He slowed down to pull into the Circle M drive. "No, I don't. But I guess I do have some issues."

That was all he said. She waited, but he didn't say more. As they got closer to Jake and Breezy's, she asked, "And they are?"

"Oh, you want to *know* my issues?"

"Yes, I do."

He reached over to turn down the radio. "I'm not very trusting. I haven't ever had a long-term relationship. I always told myself I got that from Sylvia Martin, aka Mom. I never thought I'd have kids because I didn't want to ever let a kid down. Now I think I'd like a few because if they're all like Lilly, that would be pretty amazing."

She didn't know what to say. "She is amazing. But you know, all kids are different. And you would need to get married to have more kids."

"Right, of course. I've been thinking about that."

No, not the marriage discussion. Not now. "I didn't realize it until now, but I'm starving."

"Change the subject much?"

Duke stopped the truck, and she jumped out. Before she could head for the house, he caught up with her. There was a look in his eyes that said she'd better beware. This was probably how David felt when he confronted Goliath. No, David had been confident. He'd known from the beginning that he could conquer his fears and the giant.

But the giant Oregon needed to conquer wasn't the man standing in front of her. She had other giants she needed to reserve her faith for. This man was just a distraction. A tall, devastatingly handsome distraction.

"I'm too big to brush under a rug, Oregon." He grinned. "I can't be ignored. I can't be outrun."

"Of course you can't."

He placed a sweetly chaste kiss on her lips and then backed away, just inches. "See, that wasn't so bad."

"Ewww, gross."

He laughed, and Oregon spun around to face her daughter. Before she could explain, Lilly waved her off.

"Breezy said to tell you two that lunch is ready, and the twins are hungry. And hungry twins are not a good thing."

"No, they're not." Duke hugged Lilly. "Let's see if we can help."

Lilly looked from Oregon to Duke. She looked up at the man who was her dad, acceptance written on her face. Oregon's heart eased because the look spoke of forgiveness, of getting past the anger.

Oregon followed the two of them up the front walk, her heart slowly returning to normal. She'd always known it wouldn't be easy to come here, to allow Duke in her daughter's life. But now she saw how wrong she'd been. She didn't have to fear him in her daughter's life. She had to fear him in *her* life.

She found Breezy in the kitchen. The twins were sitting in matching high chairs. The toddlers were almost identical, with dark hair and blue eyes. Rosie had always been the more vocal of the two. These days Violet seemed to be trying to catch up. When Oregon kissed Rosie on the cheek, Violet said, "Aunt Oregon."

"Oh, no." Oregon glanced at Breezy to see if she was guilty.

"Don't look at me. That's Brody's doing," Breezy said. "He's been printing wedding invitations. Something to the effect of 'Lilly

Martin would like to invite you to the wedding of her parents'."

"I'll have to hurt him," Oregon muttered as she kissed the twins, then rounded the counter to where Breezy was cutting up some herbs. "Anything I can do?"

"There isn't much left to do. Marty has the day off, but she left a salad and potato salad in the fridge. I'm just fixing up some ranch dressing." Breezy handed her a knife. "Slice tomatoes for the burgers?"

"I can do that."

Ten minutes later they were all at the table, hands held as Jake asked the blessing on the food. Duke sat across from her, and Brody sat next to him. As the food was passed around, Brody cleared his throat.

Oregon wanted to toss her knife at him. Instead, she shot the younger man a look he couldn't misinterpret. He remained unfazed.

"What?" he asked as he squeezed ketchup on his burger.

"Not funny, I think is what she wants to say." Duke grabbed the ketchup from his younger brother. "I think if you're working, you'll have less time to scheme."

"No scheming going on here." Brody started to eat.

Duke wasn't giving up. Oregon could see it in his eyes. He'd gone from teasing to serious.

"Maybe tomorrow instead of lounging around the house like you're retired at twenty-six, you ought to try helping out around here. We've got to get the hay cut and baled before that rain hits next week. And if that doesn't keep you busy, I've got a couple of geldings that we need to start working so we can put them on the website for sale."

"I'd love to help you out, but I've got an appointment in Austin."

"Is your appointment going to take all week?" Jake asked.

"Nope," Brody answered.

Oregon handed Violet a small piece of hamburger, which the little girl chomped down in three seconds flat. It was easier to handle a two-year-old than the conversation going on around them. Next to her, Lilly watched with rapt attention.

Brody finished his burger and sat back in his chair. "The invitations were a joke."

"I'm not laughing," Duke said calmly as he piled a second helping of salad on his plate.

Brody downed a glass of tea and pushed his chair away from the table. "Maybe you should laugh."

"Brody, is there something…" Breezy started. Brody cut her off with an easy look, but that look didn't quite reach his eyes.

"It's nothing, Breeze. I've got stuff to take care of."

"You wouldn't be going to have that knee checked tomorrow, would you?" Jake asked.

"Sure, that's what I'm doing."

"Need me to come along?" Jake asked as Brody headed for the door.

"Nope."

"You aren't looking for Sylvia, are you?" Duke asked.

Brody shot Duke a look. "Does it matter? It isn't like she wants to be found. Besides, she knows where we live."

"Yeah," Duke said. "She knows."

Next to Oregon, Lilly moved from her chair. As Brody limped away, Lilly asked to be excused and went after him. Oregon heard her call him Uncle Brody, asking him to wait up.

"We should just give him space, stop cornering him," Duke said.

"Yeah, I would agree if I wasn't worried about him." Jake tossed his napkin on the table. "Eventually he's going to have to tell us what's going on."

Breezy cleared her throat. "We have company, and I'm pretty sure one of you just said you should give him space. He's probably taking a walk, and Lilly is hobbling along behind him, talking his ear off and making him forget his troubles. Brody isn't a little boy who needs to be fixed. He's a grown man who's working through something in his life."

Duke and Jake remained in their seats. They gave each other a look, then went back to eating. Silence hung over the table, broken only by the occasional jabbering of the twins. Oregon wondered what it had been like in this home before Breezy came along. She knew their past had been rocky. As kids, the Martins had worked hard to keep the ranch going while they basically raised themselves. Oregon had heard the stories. Ten years ago they'd shipped their youngest sister, Samantha, off to boarding school to keep her from forming an attachment to a ranch hand. It seemed that they had a tendency to plow forward into any situation, hoping for the best.

And Oregon didn't want Duke plowing his way into her life and taking control. Somehow she'd have to make that clear to him. He was in her life for one reason, because Lilly needed him. Oregon didn't. She'd have to make the boundaries clear.

For them both.

Duke drove Oregon and Lilly down to the cottage. Lunch together had made him realize something. They were a family. A broken one, he guessed, but a family nonetheless. She was a mom. He was a dad. Lilly was their daughter.

So how did they work it out for the best? It was something they'd have to discuss. When they reached the cottage, Lilly took off for the barn and the horses that were gathered at the fence. It hadn't taken his animals long to figure out that she would give them attention. And probably an apple or two.

"She's a great kid, Oregon." He started with that. It was a simple, nonthreatening statement.

She looked up at him but kept walking, her skirt swishing around her ankles, silver hoop earrings jangling. She was tiny enough he could just scoop her up and carry her where he wanted. He grinned at the thought, because he knew if he tried any such thing, she'd fight like a wildcat.

"I'm going to make coffee." She tossed the

comment back at him. It wasn't an invitation. But at least she wasn't telling him to take a hike.

He followed Oregon inside. The house no longer felt like the place he'd lived for over six months. It didn't smell like bacon and leather. Today it smelled like spring, and like Oregon. Soft, feminine, easy to hold.

He shook his head, amazed by that thought. Half afraid of it. He glanced out the window at the girl on crutches leaning over the fence, petting the chestnut gelding he planned on giving her.

He understood that the idea of sharing her daughter didn't sit well with Oregon. He was a bachelor who hadn't given a second thought to the woman he'd met years ago.

But he was determined to make things right. Oregon filled the coffeepot with water and measured coffee into the filter basket. He studied the room, noticing the changes she'd made, the small things that were all Oregon. The scented candle on the counter, lace curtains over the window, a bouquet of flowers on the kitchen table.

He returned his attention to Oregon. She stood at the window, shoulders hunched forward, a hand to her eyes. The gesture propelled him in her direction. He didn't know what to say, so he stood behind her, wrapping his arms around her to pull her against his chest. At first she resisted, but then she softened in his arms. He bent to kiss the top of her head, and he watched out the window as she had.

Lilly stood at the fence, hugging the chestnut gelding. The sun touched her dark hair, touched the red-gold of the horse. The dogs were nearby, stretched out on the grass. This kid belonged here. Belonged to him. His heart filled up with love and pride for his daughter.

And the woman in his arms.

He dropped a kiss on the top of Oregon's head. "She's going to be okay."

"I know she is." She sobbed, and he felt a shudder go through her. "I want to know that if something should happen to me, you'll take care of her. We need to go to a lawyer and make sure she is legally yours."

He'd planned to talk about his rights and the fact that he should help support them financially. Eventually. But this was a little more serious than what he'd planned on saying right now. He stood there for a minute, still holding Oregon, her strawberry-scented hair teasing his senses, and his heart feeling like someone had just set a trap for him to fall into.

His marriage proposal that day in the hospital had been rash, and he hadn't really thought things through. Hadn't really thought about how it would make them a couple.

"Of course I'll be here for her. But I don't think we need to expect the worst."

"You never know, Duke. None of us are guaranteed tomorrow."

"No, I guess you're right." He struggled against the unsettled feeling her words evoked.

She broke away from him and leaned back against the counter to look up at him. With a trembling hand, she brushed a strand of hair from her eyes. "I'm sorry, Duke. I know that you know way too much about lives lost too soon. I just need to know that you're ready to be a dad. I don't want Lilly to have a part-time father. I want her to have the real thing, because it matters."

"I know it does. But I'm not going anywhere. Neither are you, for that matter. I want time with Lilly. I want to teach her to ride, and someday teach her to drive. I want to scare those boys that try to date her. I want to be there when she gets married. And I'm pretty sure I owe you some support."

She swiped at the tears streaming down her cheeks. He pulled a tissue from the box on the counter and pushed it into her hand. She thanked him and wiped her eyes.

"I'm sorry I waited so long to tell you. I planned it out, knew what had to be said, and then didn't know how to do it. I just…didn't want her to go through what I did as a kid."

"Don't worry. I'm not walking out on her. And I hope you're not leaving town with her."

"I'm not going anywhere."

"Now maybe we could discuss that horse out there she's petting."

That distracted her from the thoughts that were putting those tears in her eyes. She glared at him. "What have you done?"

"I bought my kid her first pony. Well, not really a pony."

"Duke, you know how I feel about this."

He shrugged it off. "Yeah, I know you want her to earn the money. Don't worry. She'll have to continue to earn the horse by doing chores."

"And you get to be the hero."

"No, we'll both be the hero. Let's do this together, Oregon. Let's give our kid a horse. We'll make the rules together. That's how we'll parent her. Together. If that's acceptable to you. If not, we'll do something else."

It took a minute but she finally nodded, agreeing to his plan. "Okay, we'll let her work for the horse you've bought. But next time, we talk before you make the decision to buy."

"Next time I talk to you before, not after."

Her smile returned, lighting up her gray eyes and doing something to his heart. "You're going to be a good dad, Duke."

He couldn't have agreed more. Oregon wasn't thinking about worst case scenarios for the first time in probably a long time. And Lilly would have the best quarter horse around.

Not too shabby for his first week as a dad.

Chapter Eight

Business on Monday morning was brisk at the diner. Duke had sent out more plates of biscuits and gravy than he could count, and someone had just ordered pie. He slid the slice of chocolate pie onto a plate and rang the bell. Ned gave him a grin and a shake of her head as she picked up the order and headed back out the door. Duke wiped the sweat from his face with a towel and took a moment to breathe. No orders waiting for him. The rush was over. At least for the time being.

He wiped down the stainless-steel counter, put eggs in the cooler and poured himself a cup of coffee as he glanced at the clock.

A moment later Ned walked through the kitchen door. She sighed big and then mumbled something about how people ought to tip once in a while. Duke glanced her way. She had poured herself a cup of coffee and she took a long drink, obviously not caring how hot it might be.

"Boss, are you doing okay?" she asked as she settled on a stool by the sink.

"Not bad, Ned. Are the customers stiffing you again?"

She shrugged and took another sip. "Not too bad. I know times are tough."

"Yeah, but I'm not going to let you work for free."

"I'm not working for free. And you have a daughter to think about now."

"Yeah, a daughter." He leaned against the counter. "Life changes so fast."

"Yeah, not a month ago she was that cute kid of Oregon's. Now she's your daughter. That changes everything."

"Don't I know it, Ned."

It changed his outlook, his feelings, his future.

"I'm going to take a lap through the dining room and talk to customers. Why don't you eat?" he offered.

"I think I'll do that." She hopped down from the stool, spry for her age and size.

He admired Ned. She could wrangle cattle,

break a horse and take care of his entire dining room alone if she had to. He refilled his coffee cup and headed out of the kitchen.

As he walked into the dining room, Boone Wilder waved from the far corner booth. Next to him, Daron McKay nodded. The young woman sitting with them looked familiar, but he couldn't place her. He grabbed a chair from another table and sat at the end of the booth.

"What brings you all to town?" he asked, leaning his chair back on two legs.

"Business," Boone answered.

Duke nodded. Boone had mentioned a business idea to him recently, something about bodyguards. Duke guessed it was really just three friends who'd done a tour in Afghanistan together trying to figure out how to stay in each other's lives and stay sane. He understood. Cooking had been his sanity.

Daron pushed his plate back. Daron McKay's dad had a law firm in Austin. They had a hobby farm outside Martin's Crossing. A few nice horses, some cattle and a lot of society friends who liked to come down for weekends. It wasn't Duke's crowd.

"I need to head out. Boone, we'll talk later in the week," the young woman said as she tossed a few dollars on the table. "That should cover my coffee."

"Sounds good." Boone, raised old-fashioned, stood as she slid out of the booth.

She smiled at Duke, the kind of smile that definitely didn't settle in her dark eyes. "Mr. Martin, good to see you."

He put a finger to his brow in a salute.

Boone sat back down, reaching for his coffee as he did.

"Lucy isn't charming, but she's tough," Daron said. "Good breakfast this morning, Duke."

Duke moved his chair back to the table it'd come from and sat in the booth opposite Boone and Daron. "Lucy looks familiar."

"Her dad was Paulo Palermo," Daron answered.

"Died on a bull a few years ago, didn't he?" Duke asked. The two men nodded. "So you're serious about this business."

"Serious as we can be," Daron answered. "How's your little girl doing? Recovering from the accident?"

Duke nearly spilled his coffee. His little girl. It still unsettled him when people mentioned it. He tried to pretend interest in whatever he saw outside the window. Instead, he relived the accident in his mind. The moment the car touched her body and she went down. He'd been standing outside waiting for her, because he'd felt protective of her from the day she first walked through the doors of the diner.

It all felt different now somehow, because it hadn't happened to a stranger. It had been his daughter, his little girl, on the pavement in front of that car.

"Duke, you okay?" Boone asked.

Duke shook free from his thoughts. "Yeah, I'm good. Thanks for asking. She's much better. I gave her a horse yesterday."

Boone chuckled at that. "Nice."

"How are your folks doing?" Duke said, changing the conversation to something a little easier to handle. For him. Boone shrugged and shook his head at the question.

"Broke. They're buying back some cattle, but it hasn't been easy. Dad is better, though, so that makes all the difference."

Boone's dad had suffered a major heart attack, and they'd nearly lost everything. Duke guessed that's why the younger man wanted to start a business.

"Glad to hear that." Duke looked out the window again. Oregon had wandered out of her shop to hang something on the outside of the building. Lilly stood next to her, swinging back and forth on the crutches.

A moment later Joe came down the sidewalk, stopping to talk to them. Duke had always heard fatherhood changed a man. He guessed that had to be right, because for the first time he cared about who Joe Anderson might be, and why he'd stayed in Martin's Crossing.

"Problem?" Daron asked.

"No, just…" What did he say? He suddenly had suspicions for no good reason? "It's just… Do you guys ever wonder who Joe is, where he came from?"

"Hasn't everyone?" Boone answered with casual indifference. "They ran Joe Anderson through the computer and came up with nothing."

"Maybe that isn't his name."

"Wow, suspicious all of a sudden?" Boone said. "I don't think he'd hurt that little girl, if that's what you're thinking."

"I guess it is."

A daughter changed a man, made him more careful, less trusting. Besides, Joe had taken to leaving town for a couple of days at a time.

He didn't say much about where he was going or when he'd be back.

"We should be going," Boone said. "We have an appointment in Austin."

Boone slid out of the booth and Daron followed.

"I'll walk you out," Duke offered, his thoughts still distracted. A little fresh air might help.

As they walked out the door of the diner, warm air welcomed them. Duke took off his hat and brushed a hand through his hair. Daron and Boone didn't make a move to leave.

Across the street Oregon stood on a step stool, and Lilly handed her a pretty glass globe. His gaze settled on Oregon. She wore a pretty sundress, bright colors all swirled together. Her hair was pulled back from her face. She reached up to adjust the string that held the globe. He should go over and offer to help. Not that she'd want it.

But he wouldn't mind standing close to her, holding the ladder so she didn't fall. He shook his head. She'd lived across the street from his diner for the past year, and suddenly he'd gone from casual observer of his pretty neighbor to a man who wouldn't mind walking across the street and taking her in his arms.

A year, or even six months ago, he hadn't known she could bring a sense of peace to his heart. He hadn't known how holding her would shift things inside him.

Just then, Boone Wilder cleared his throat. Duke glared at him. "Need anything else, Boone?"

Boone pushed the cowboy hat down on his head and raised a brow. "Yeah, actually. You know, we could do a little digging and find out who Joe is. Something tells me you'd rest a little easier knowing the truth."

"And how are we going to do that digging?"

Boone's gaze shifted across the street, and Duke followed that casual glance. Lilly had rounded the side of a building, and Joe pointed at something in the eaves. Probably a bird's nest.

"I have a friend. He used to be a state trooper, and now he's a PI. He might dig something up," Daron offered.

It only took Duke a minute of watching his daughter with Joe to make a decision. "Yeah, tell him to dig."

Boone nodded, and Daron tipped his hat. The two said their goodbyes and headed down the steps. At the same time Lilly crossed the street, beaming from ear to ear. When she got to the diner steps, she shifted the crutches out from under her arms and hopped, using the rail to make her way up.

"Your mom is watching," he warned when she reached his side.

"Yeah, but she wouldn't want to try those steps with crutches, either. Besides, they're going to give me a walking cast soon."

"Yeah, but she also doesn't want you to break your other leg."

She rolled her eyes as she placed the crutches back under her arms. "I came to sweep the deck. It's probably going to be a busy lunch crowd and since it's not too hot, people might want to sit outside."

"Sweep, huh?"

"I can do it."

"Of course you can." They both walked inside.

"I have a horse to earn." She grinned big. It was the same grin he'd seen yesterday when they told her the gelding was hers on the condition that she continue to do chores. She'd hugged Oregon first, then she'd hugged him. It had felt like the best day of his life.

"Mom said I could stay with you sometime. If you want."

"Did she?"

She rolled her eyes. "You're my dad, right? That's what kids do. They stay with their dads. Well, some kids live with their moms and dads. But I'm okay with having you down the road. That's better than not having you at all."

He didn't know what to say.

"Are you going to pass out?" Lilly asked as she reached for the broom.

Standing in the kitchen, she watched him, concern in her big blue eyes. He looked from her to the broom. How was she going to sweep?

"No, I don't pass out. And I don't see how you can do this."

She sighed, hopping past him on one crutch, the broom in her hand. "I'm getting pretty good on these."

"Yes, you are. But be careful." She shook her head at him as she went out the door.

He followed Lilly outside. If she insisted on doing this, he would keep an eye on her. He carried her other crutch and watched her as she started to sweep.

"What's your mom doing today?" He looked from his daughter to the shop across the street. Oregon had gone back inside.

Lilly kept sweeping. "She doesn't feel good. She said maybe it's a stomach virus. She's sitting in the back room sewing skirts and hoping no one comes in."

"Does she need anything?"

"No, she just wants to be alone. But I'm worried. She was like this last year when she got sick."

"She got sick last year?" He pushed himself off the rail and walked down the length of deck to where Lilly was sweeping. He rested the forgotten crutch against the rail so she could grab it if needed.

Lilly stopped sweeping to face him. "Yeah, before we moved here. It was just a virus, but it took her a long time to get over it."

"Is that when you stayed with friends for a month?"

She nodded. "But it wasn't because she was sick. They had a ranch and horses. I think my grandma was married to Pamela's dad once, and she and my mom have stayed friends."

"Gotcha. So you're okay here? I think I'll go check and see if your mom needs tea or maybe soup."

"She won't, but go ahead." She swept a few more strokes and stopped again. "It worries me when she's sick because she looks worried."

He kissed the top of his daughter's head.

"You don't have to worry. You're not alone. Your mom isn't alone."

"Yeah, I know. But we've always kind of taken care of each other."

"And now there are three of us to take care of each other." He handed her the other crutch. "Take a break. Ned will make you a shake."

Her smile returned, bright and sweet. "Thanks."

He watched her go inside before he bounded down the steps and headed for Oregon's All Things, the shop she'd opened when she came to town. He walked through the front door, the bell ringing lightly. The room smelled of apple pie, courtesy of the candle on the counter. Oregon didn't greet him. He walked to the back of the shop and knocked on the door to her apartment.

A faint "One moment" was her only answer.

He didn't feel like waiting. Instead, he pushed the door open and invaded her space. Because if she was sick, she didn't need space. She needed help.

She needed him.

Oregon opened her eyes when the door opened. She should have known it would be him. She didn't know if she should be angry or thankful at his invasion.

"You're sick?" he asked as he hovered over her, a great hulk of a man with broad shoulders a woman could lean on, and concern shadowing his blue eyes like she meant something to him.

"It's just a virus. Did Lilly come over and make a bigger deal out of this than it is?"

"She's worried about you. She said the last time you were sick you sent her away for a month."

"It wasn't like that. I had a virus, and it took me a while to get over it. But Pamela wanted her for a month that summer."

He placed his large hand on her forehead. "No fever."

She closed her eyes at the cool touch of his hand, shivering when he brushed fingers down her cheek. "Please sit down. You're looming. It makes me feel a little overwhelmed."

"I want to know the truth."

"The truth is, I think I ate something that disagreed with me, and you and Lilly are making a big deal out of nothing." She smiled at him, hoping she looked convincing. She was fine. No need to worry.

If only she could believe that herself.

"You know I'm here if you need anything?"

"Yes, I know. I appreciate that. But I really don't need anything."

"Tea? Crackers?"

"I have ginger tea, and I'm not really hungry."

He leaned toward her, his elbows resting on his knees as he studied her. She glanced away, because she didn't want him to look too closely. She didn't want him to see her fear. She didn't want him to see the emotions she barely understood or recognized. Because she needed him in ways she hadn't expected.

Being here, so close to him, she realized that he made her feel safe. He made her feel protected. She tried to think of any other man who had ever done that for her.

There hadn't been any. Not one.

It wasn't fair. It shouldn't be this man. Not now. A tear slid down her cheek. She brushed it away, turning from him so that he wouldn't see.

But he did see. His hand traced the damp path of the tear. He mumbled something and suddenly she was in his arms, held against him. She wanted to fight the embrace, but she couldn't. His arms felt too good, too strong and comforting to fight.

"Just tell me what I can do."

"There's nothing you can do. I'm…" She prayed she wasn't lying. "I'm fine."

"Of course you are." He held her tight, and she curled into him until she realized what she was doing.

She pulled herself together and moved out of his arms. "I am."

He grinned, and her heart unfortunately somersaulted. "Let me take you to the doctor."

"No, thank you. If I need to go to the doctor, I'll go. But I don't."

"Okay, no doctor. Go home for the day. Lilly is fine with me. You can sleep, rest up for your mom's visit, and I'll bring dinner later."

She wanted to tell him she could take care of herself. After all, she'd been doing just that for years. She'd taken care of herself and Lilly. She'd made it through the best and worst of times alone.

Alone. She squeezed her eyes shut and remembered the day Lilly was born. Oregon had been alone with just a nurse to hold her hand, offering to call someone for her, anyone.

She could have called her mom, but Eugenia had been in California, and Oregon had been in Oklahoma. Duke had been long gone.

But he was here now.

"I'll drive you home."

"I'm fine. Really." But a sudden pain in her abdomen took her breath away.

"That's it. We're going home. Now." He pulled keys from his pocket. "Let's go. Lilly can stay with Ned while we're gone."

"But…"

He placed a finger on her lips to stop her from speaking.

"Do *not* argue with me."

He scooped her into his arms, holding her as easily as he would hold a child. He carried her out the back door to the parking lot. People stared. Of course they did. She shut her eyes so that she wouldn't have to see who all witnessed her humiliation.

She didn't want anyone to watch her fall. She couldn't fall. Not in love. She couldn't imagine trusting someone with her heart, trusting that he wouldn't leave. She couldn't imagine anyone loving her enough to want to stay in her life.

"Here we are." His words vibrated against her, and he reached to open the truck door. With careful ease he sat her in the truck. "Stay. I'll be right back."

"Bossy man."

"You'd better believe it."

Oregon watched him cross the road to the restaurant. He spoke to Lilly, who glanced toward the truck, and even from a distance Oregon saw the worried frown on her daughter's face. That was the last thing she wanted. A daughter shouldn't have to worry about her mother. She should be carefree, playing with friends, talking about boys. All of the things girls did at that age. The last thing Oregon wanted for her daughter was to have her become the adult in their relationship. Oregon had lived that childhood. She wouldn't let that happen to Lilly. Ever.

Duke returned, opened the driver's-side door and got behind the wheel. "You okay?"

"I'm good."

"Do you need anything before we leave town?" He started the truck and pulled onto the road.

"I can't think of anything."

Duke drove her home in silence. When they pulled up to the little house she'd managed to turn into a home in the past week, she knew that Duke would try to carry her again. She couldn't let him. She was strong enough to walk. But her heart wasn't strong enough to endure his chivalrous, cowboy nature. Before he could reach her, she was out and on her own two feet, proving that she was just fine.

She drew in a deep breath and headed for the house, telling herself she really was fine. The virus would pass in a day or two, and she would be back to normal.

"Let me settle you on the sofa, maybe get you a cup of mint tea." Duke opened the front door for her.

Oregon chuckled.

"What's so funny?" He grabbed pillows and plumped them on the sofa.

"You, hovering like a nursemaid and offering mint tea. I'm picturing you in a nurse's cap, or with an apron."

He covered her with an afghan and for a moment she held her breath, thinking he would kiss her. She wanted that kiss. Then she didn't. Not today, when her heart might make more of a kiss than it actually meant. Fortunately, he backed away, and the moment evaporated like mist in the morning sun.

"I'm very secure in my manhood. Secure enough to make mint tea."

She touched his hand, letting her fingers briefly curl in his. "Your secret is safe with me."

He winked and walked away, leaving her

to dangerous thoughts about him. She closed her eyes and prayed, because God had gotten her this far. He wouldn't leave her now.

to dangers she didn't know about him. She doesn't
love you and you're going to want to God had gotten
her this far. He would take care of the rest.

Chapter Nine

The next day, Oregon felt better. She convinced herself it really had been a virus, nothing more. Nothing to fear. As she walked through the doors of her shop, she said a silent prayer of thanks. Because for a day or two she had started to doubt everything God had done for her. And He had done so much. She had this shop, a business that was beginning to prosper. She had Lilly.

She wasn't going to take any of it, not one thing, not one person, not one day, for granted. She shoved her purse under a table in the back room and dragged out the new shelves she planned on hanging. Lilly came in through the front door, a grin on her face.

"Guess who's here?" Lilly asked, holding the door open with the tip of a crutch.

"I have no idea." But her heart sank, thinking it might be her mother early.

"Brody." Lilly moved forward, and Brody stepped in behind her.

"I saw you carrying in something that looked like a project," he said with a casual shrug.

Carefree, that's what everyone thought of Brody Martin. Oregon didn't agree. He wanted them all to think that nothing bothered him. But she saw the shadows in his blue eyes. Brody had a lot on his mind.

"I'm putting up new shelves," she admitted. "I have a few new items that I need space for."

"I can help," he offered. "I've obviously just been sitting around for months, so I should probably find something to do."

Oregon touched his arm briefly. Brody didn't look like a man needing to be comforted. He looked like a man trying to find his place in the world. "Is there anything…"

He cut her off. "Oh, don't worry about me, Oregon. I'm just going through growing pains, trying to convince my brothers to stop treating me like a kid."

"I know it isn't easy. They're…"

"Overbearing?" he suggested.

"Sometimes. But they mean well." She

poured a cup of coffee and offered him one. He shook his head.

"No coffee for me. But if you show me where you want these shelves, I'd be happy to help out."

Lilly had wandered outside when the conversation had turned serious. She returned to watch as they dragged the lumber and the brackets to the front of the store. Oregon had painted the wood white, giving it a country look that she hoped would work with the rest of the store.

As they were measuring where the shelves would be placed, the front door of the shop opened, the bell tinkling softly. Joe stepped in, and his face lit up when he spotted Lilly.

"There's our girl," he said. "How are you doing, sweet pea?"

Oregon glanced from Joe to her daughter, who beamed at the nickname he'd bestowed on her almost from the beginning of their relationship. When he'd first arrived in town, Oregon had been cautious of Joe. But he'd been in town since late last fall, and he'd become a big part of the church and their community.

"I'm good. A little bored." Lilly scooted around a display case to meet Joe in the center of the store. "I can't swim. Or even ride a horse. I wanted to learn to ride this summer."

"Oh, it'll get easier. And time will fly by. I think it won't be long before you'll be doing all of that fun stuff."

"Yeah, probably." Her agreement wasn't wholehearted.

Joe only smiled. "How is that horse fund going?"

At that she perked up. "Duke gave me a horse. I still have to work for it, and I can't ride him until my cast is off, but his name is Chief, and he's beautiful."

"I'd like to see him sometime."

"Yeah, maybe you can come out some night this week. My grandma is coming in. Well, she doesn't like to be called Grandma. I call her JeanJean."

"Oh, I see." Joe went a little pale. Mention of her mother could do that to people. "Well, I'd love to do that. But I might be gone for a week or so. Maybe your grandmother will still be here when I get back?"

Lilly shook her head. "No, she won't stay long."

"Well, maybe next time." Joe touched Lilly's head, smoothing her dark hair. Oregon noticed the light going out of his eyes. "I'll see you soon."

He said his goodbyes and walked down the sidewalk.

"Odd old man," Brody muttered as he went back to work on the brackets for the shelves.

"But kind." Oregon watched out the window as Joe reached the end of the block. He turned east, and she wondered where he was headed.

Lilly moved over to the window, watching as kids raced down the road on bikes, probably heading to the park. The girl let out a forlorn sigh. Oregon patted her back as she walked past her to rejoin Brody at the shelving. She knew that nothing she could say would change how Lilly felt.

"I want something to do." Lilly joined Oregon and Brody, leaning forward on the crutches and swinging a little.

"Don't fall. That's something you can do for me." Oregon handed the shortest board to Brody, and he lifted it to put it on the top brackets.

"But I'm bored," Lilly continued.

"You could read a book or watch television," Oregon said.

"Go see what your dad is up to. Maybe he has something you can do," Brody offered.

Oregon's heart stopped at the word *dad*. She glanced at Lilly and saw her stricken, wide-eyed look. That three-letter word had changed all of their lives but it wasn't the word Lilly used for Duke. Not yet.

Brody turned to look at them, his eyes narrowing a little. "What?"

Lilly just looked at him.

"He is your dad, right?" Brody said.

"Yeah, he is." Lilly bit down on her bottom lip. Oregon waited. "Sometimes it doesn't seem real. He's still just Duke to me."

"I get that. I'm sure if I ever find my mom, it won't seem real, either. And I've always known she existed."

They were quite a trio, Oregon decided. Brody, always wondering where his mother was. Lilly just learning she had a father. And Oregon never knowing who her father was.

"So I guess I could go see if he has something for me to do, since I can't ride bikes or anything," Lilly said, looking totally unsure. Was she waiting for Oregon to object?

"Sure you can," Oregon said. "If you decide to stay over there, call and let me know."

"Thanks, Mom." Lilly hugged her, then she was gone.

After she'd left, Brody patted Oregon awkwardly on the arm. "You aren't losing her, you know."

"I know." She pinched the bridge of her nose until the sting left her eyes. "Okay, let's get back to work."

When she opened her eyes, Brody was watching her.

"He's going to be a good dad." Brody reached for the second board. "He used to be pretty wild, but he's settled down and knows how to be there for a person."

"I know you're right, but it isn't easy."

"No, I guess it wouldn't be." He situated the shelf in place. "Do you think I'm crazy, trying to find Sylvia?"

His mother. She shook her head. "No, I think you have questions, and only she can supply the answers."

They were placing the last shelf on the wall when the door opened. Duke ducked his head to enter the shop.

"I have to run errands, then do some work out at the ranch. Lilly wants to go with me, if you don't mind."

For a brief moment she hesitated. She knew

they were going to do things together. Without her. But this was different than Lilly running across the street to Duke's. Every day they were taking steps further into each other's lives. Oregon had even agreed that Lilly could sometimes stay at Duke's house.

She nodded, letting go of the need to hold Lilly close. "Yes, of course. I'll be home later."

"I'll cook dinner," Duke said as he walked out the door.

"Thank you."

Oregon watched as he got in his truck. From the passenger-side window, Lilly waved a happy goodbye. This was one thing in her life she didn't have to worry about. She only had to let go and trust.

Duke paused in the center of the corral to adjust the stirrup that held his daughter's foot, and then walked to the other side to the makeshift stirrup he'd created for her cast. Yeah, it probably wasn't the best idea. But Lilly had been waiting a long time for this horse.

He didn't realize he'd been waiting a long time for her. He patted her knee and looked up at her. She beamed, like the happiest kid in the world. She didn't know it, but she was making him about the happiest man. This kid and her mom were putting back the pieces of him that he'd thought were missing for good.

Each day he felt a little more hopeful. He'd had fewer nightmares of late, too. He was able to face God without the anger of the past few years. Yeah, life was pretty good.

In the distance he heard a car coming up the road. He knew it was Oregon. Lilly groaned, "Oh, no."

"We're in trouble now," Duke said as he led the gelding around the corral. But it wasn't just Lilly in the saddle that was going to cause Oregon some stress. The woman sitting on the patio would probably be Oregon's worst nightmare. Her mother had been there an hour. *Pleasant* hadn't been the right word to describe her.

"Should I get down?" Lilly asked.

"I don't see a reason to go running now. She's seen us. Now we just have to defend our position."

"Good luck with that," Lilly said in a loud whisper. "She's mad."

He braved a look in Oregon's direction as she got out of her car. Yes, that was one unhappy woman.

He led the horse through the gate and toward Oregon. She now stood in front of her car, arms crossed over her chest. She looked from him to her daughter on the back of the gelding. A breeze kicked up, blowing strands of dark hair across her cheek. She brushed them back with an impatient gesture.

Something about her anger made him a little unsettled. Not in a bad way. No, sir. He wanted to kiss that frown off her face. He brightened at the thought and she probably noticed. Which was probably why her frown grew.

"*This* is what you call being responsible?" Oregon accused.

"No, this is what I call spending an afternoon teaching my daughter how to ride."

Daughter. Dad. Duke loved using those words. He hadn't expected to feel this way. He had never expected to want this. Man, he loved his daughter. He grinned a little more, but after looking at Oregon, the smile dissolved.

Her expression was a real mixture of anger and concern and fear.

"She's safe, Oregon. I wouldn't do anything to hurt her. I've had the lead rope the entire time. And Chief is as gentle as they come."

"I'm sure he is." Oregon's gaze shot past

him to the car with Florida tags. "I guess this is the least of my worries."

"Yeah, I thought about warning you." He moved a little closer but stayed near the horse and near Lilly.

It felt a lot like shielding her. If he stood there, it would keep her from the woman who had a tendency to unsettle her world. It would make her feel safe.

"She shouldn't be on a horse, Duke." Oregon's arms dropped to her sides, and she looked just about defeated. And there was something in her eyes that said more. He shouldn't be giving Lilly this moment, not without Oregon.

He considered telling Oregon she'd had a lot of firsts, too. He'd missed out on twelve years of firsts. Now wasn't the time to go there. Nothing would get him back those twelve years.

"She's safe. I'm right here if anything happened."

"Yes, I know. I'm sorry." She let out a ragged sigh. "If you can help her down, I'll go speak to my mother."

"Wait a minute, and we'll all go together." He extended the support like a peace offering, hoping it would soothe her.

"Yes, well…" Eugenia stood and started walking their way. "Never mind, she's coming to us."

As if she didn't understand the turmoil she caused, Oregon's mom headed toward them. When she reached them, she embraced Oregon tightly. Duke got wrapped up in a cloud of perfume and nearly choked. Eugenia Jeffries was a combination of copper-colored hair, pale face and clothes meant for a woman decades younger.

"Oregon, honey, I'm so glad to see you. You look wonderful. So healthy. But a little pale. Are you feeling okay?"

"Mom, you just said I look healthy." Oregon slipped from her mother's embrace.

"Well, yes, healthy but pale. I don't know, maybe it's just the stress of dealing with these Martins. They do tend to take over, and they will not listen when a person tries to reason with them."

"Mom…"

"I'm just saying, I told him not to put my granddaughter on a horse. He insisted he knows what he's doing. But isn't that just how they are? They think they run this town."

"Mom!" Oregon tried again. Duke was ready to send her mother packing.

"Oh, don't worry. I'm not here to cause problems. I get it. They don't want to hear my opinions about their church and their community events. I'm just saying, they should try to be more inclusive."

"The way you are when you insist that everyone bend to your will? Change their beliefs to suit you?" Oregon rushed the words out, and Duke wanted to hug her. "Mom, just stop. Please. Come in, have dinner with us."

Eugenia threw her hands up in the air, bracelets jangling. "Yes, of course. Whatever you want."

"That's what I want. I want peace."

"I'm just here to help you out. And I brought Lilly a gift. I brought it in the house while she was riding. I didn't want her to see it until you got home."

"Oh, the surprise. I forgot." Oregon looked less than thrilled. She looked up at her daughter, still sitting on her horse, then at Duke. "You should probably help her down while we go inside."

"Her crutches are in the barn. We'll be up at the house in a few minutes." Duke rested a hand on the horse's neck.

Standing in the yard, Duke watched her walk away, Eugenia talking nonstop about something. He glanced up at Lilly, and she shook her head.

"She's always like this," Lilly said. "She just takes over and does what she wants."

"Yeah, I've kind of noticed. Let's hurry so we can rescue your mom."

"Yeah, she always makes Mom feel bad about something."

So they hurried. He unsaddled the horse, handing Lilly a brush to use on the animal while he put the tack away. She leaned on one crutch and smoothed the brush over the horse's neck and back. He watched them together and for a minute forgot the tornado of a woman in the house.

But he couldn't forget for very long. They were almost to the door of the house when he heard raised voices from inside. But he didn't quite catch the words.

"I don't know why you thought it necessary to bring her here," Eugenia said. "And put that man in her life. Men take over and start making decisions. They don't care what you want."

"Like you, Mom? You've always made decisions based on what *you* wanted, never what I wanted or needed. This is *my* life, *my* child, and I'm doing what I think is right for her."

"Oh, you're still mad because I won't tell

you who your father is. You should thank me. He's a drunk. Nothing but a drunk. You're better off without him."

"Why can't you let me make that decision?" Oregon's voice rose a notch, taking on steely resolve. Duke wanted to cheer her on, but Lilly was next to him, wide-eyed and listening. "Let's have a sit on the patio."

A minute later the door opened. Oregon walked out, running a hand through her hair and taking several deep breaths. Duke got up from the patio table and headed her way. She saw him and offered a tight smile. There wasn't much to the gesture. It didn't say that everything would be okay. It was one of those looks a person pasted on when they wanted to fool people.

It didn't fool him.

"She bought my daughter a bird. One that talks. It's huge and has a messy cage," Oregon told him.

"That makes me feel better about the horse," he teased, hoping to ease the tension.

"Yes, the horse now looks like the best gift ever."

"Not a gift. She has to work for it."

Oregon's hand reached for his. "Thank you."

"No problem. Saving damsels in distress is

my job." He gave her hand a gentle squeeze. "And I made you dinner."

"I think I lo…" She stopped, and a stricken look settled on her face. "I…I…"

He did his best to lighten the mood. "Of course you love me. Who doesn't?"

"My grandma, obviously," Lilly said with a smirk as she walked past them on her way inside. "I'm going to see this bird."

Oregon cleared her throat, the corners of her mouth tugging up. "So what's for dinner?"

"Pulled pork sandwiches with my home-made BBQ sauce, potato salad and baked beans."

"Perfect." She came in close to his side. "A man who rescues damsels, then cooks for them."

"Yep. Easy to love."

She didn't reply. But even in her silence, he felt hopeful. He was an optimist, after all. Maybe even a man of faith.

Chapter Ten

The soldier on the ground cried for his mom. He wasn't young, maybe midtwenties. But when they were wounded, they were all kids. They all still begged for their mom or dad, their wife. Duke tried his best to comfort him. Tried to tell him it would be okay, he'd make it to the hospital, and they'd save him. But the private kept telling him it wasn't going to help. It was no use.

Duke couldn't accept that. He kept trying. The sound of helicopters pounded in his ears, and wind swept across the terrain. It wouldn't be long. Suddenly the ground where the soldier had just lain was empty, and the helicopter had disappeared.

Duke woke with a start, his heart racing. He swung his legs over the edge of the bed

and sat up. Sick to his stomach and soaked
in sweat, he buried his face in his hands. He
glanced at the clock on the night table. It was
just past four in the morning. For a minute he
sat there trying to force the dream from his
mind. It had been a while since he'd had that
nightmare.

As his heart settled into a near-normal pace,
he decided he might as well get out of bed because he knew he wouldn't be able to go back
to sleep. He splashed cold water on his face,
got dressed and headed down the stairs. There
was only one way to clear his head. He would
go for an early-morning run before he took
care of livestock. Today was his day off from
the diner. So much for sleeping in.

The air hadn't cooled much overnight, but
it still felt better than it would when the sun
came up. He headed down the driveway. If
he ran to the main, then back and to the barn
twice, he would run almost two miles. The
dogs Daisy and Belle joined him. Daisy only
stayed with him part of the way, stopping
at Jake's place to go lie on the porch. Belle
stayed with him the whole time.

On his second lap Belle gave up and joined
Daisy on Jake's porch. Duke kept pushing,

focusing on his steps, on breathing, on anything but that nightmare.

When he got to the barn the second time, he slowed, stretching his arms over his head as he walked, breathing deep. Belle and Daisy ran past him, chasing something through the brush behind the barn.

"Duke?" The timid voice came from behind him. He turned, and it was Lilly, her dark hair pulled back in a braid.

"What are you doing up?"

"I heard a noise, and when I looked out, I saw you jogging."

"You should go back to bed, kiddo."

She made a face, and he realized how much she looked like his sister, Samantha. "I can't sleep. I thought maybe something was wrong."

"No, nothing is wrong." He walked with her back to the house. As they got to the patio, the porch light came on, and Oregon opened the back door. She peered into the darkness, standing there in sweats and a T-shirt, her hair pulled back in a ponytail.

"Something wrong?"

He shook his head. "No, there's nothing wrong. I woke Lilly up."

"I was already awake," his daughter grumbled as she walked through the door.

"Go back to bed." Oregon kissed Lilly's cheek and brushed a hand down her arm.

"I still think something's wrong," Lilly continued as she walked farther into the house.

Duke didn't know what to say. He stood on the patio watching Oregon as she followed their daughter back inside. Now would be the time to make his escape.

He turned to walk away when the door opened again. It was Oregon, handing him a bottle of water, her mouth lifting in a shy, questioning smile.

"You're not okay," she said as she walked past him to the glider, where she sat down. She drew her legs up, wrapping her arms around them and pulling them in close.

He downed the bottle of water, then he sat next to her. She didn't push for an answer. He appreciated that, because he didn't have answers. He had doubts. He had anger. But answers were hard to find. He looked up at the sky, still inky black and full of stars. Somewhere in the distance a coyote howled.

Somewhere out there, maybe as distant as the stars or as close as the air he breathed, God existed. He had always believed. Maybe he hadn't been the best sheep in the fold, but he'd gone to church, he'd prayed and he'd trusted that God would always be there to rescue him.

He'd come to realize that God had rescued him. He'd sent a lifeline in the form of a twelve-year-old girl and a woman who possessed the ability to wait for a man to gather his thoughts.

"Nightmares," he finally admitted into the silence. He crushed the empty bottle and held it, staring at the label.

"Want to talk about it?"

He never talked about it. But she looked at him, her gray eyes shadowed in the pale early-morning light. She was easy to be around. And it felt good that she cared enough to ask him. It wasn't like when he'd first come home and needed space. He'd brushed off the questions. Everyone had wanted to know if he was okay, and how bad it had been over there. Eventually his family, the people in town, they'd all learned to leave him alone. They'd stopped asking questions. He'd once heard Jake say that he would work through it in his own way and in his own time.

He had been working through it. He'd built a business, helped take care of the Circle M and he'd remembered each of those young men he'd lost. He'd written down their names, the ones he could remember.

He'd yelled at God. A lot. A long time ago Pastor Allen had knocked on his door and given Duke the advice that it was okay to be mad, but eventually he would know when it was time to let it go.

"Duke?" Oregon leaned her shoulder against his.

"There isn't a lot to tell. The dreams are always the same. I'm back in Afghanistan, and I can't save anyone. Help never gets there in time."

Her hand closed over his. "I'm sorry."

"Me, too."

"Do you ever think about the ones you saved?"

"No, I guess I don't," he admitted.

"Maybe you should think of those men, too."

"Yeah." They sat there for a long time, just holding hands, letting dawn chase away the darkness.

"I'm taking the day off," she told him after they'd sat there awhile. "Can Lilly stay with you for a few hours?"

"Where are you going?"

"I have to run to Austin to deliver a few orders and check on some things." She didn't give more details. He wanted to push, but he didn't.

"What about your mom?"

"She's leaving this morning. Someone to see in Colorado, and then she's going on to California. I knew she wouldn't stay long. One night surprises me, but it doesn't matter."

He couldn't tell if she was hurt or relieved. Maybe both.

"I'm off today. I could go with you to Austin. We could all go," he offered.

"No." She stood, slipping her hand from his, her fingers brushing his palm as she did. "I don't want to drag Lilly to town. We have to go next week for her checkup. You can come then."

"What day?"

"Wednesday."

"Sounds good." He wished he could reach for her one last time. But he didn't. The sun was starting to rise. It wouldn't be long before the day started to heat up. "I have to get some work done around here. Ned is opening for me this morning."

"You're sure it won't be a problem for Lilly to stay here?"

"It won't be a problem. If she gets tired of following me around, she can stay with Breezy."

She nodded. "I'll have her get ready."

They stood there, facing each other for a long moment, as he tried to convince himself he should walk away. It made him feel a little better that she didn't seem to be in a hurry to walk away, either. He closed the distance between them, drawn to her warmth, her calm presence. He tangled his fingers with hers and brought her hand to his lips. He dropped a kiss on the back of her hand, knowing it wouldn't be enough.

He wondered if he could ever have enough of her in his world. He considered telling her that, but he knew she'd spook the minute the words were out. If he had any sense, he'd walk away. The Duke of six months ago would have.

Maybe. Or maybe not.

Walking away was a lot more difficult when this woman stood in front of him. Still holding her hand he brushed his lips against hers in a light kiss. He needed to memorize her. He settled his lips against hers.

Her hand rested on his chest. She broke the kiss, whispering that they shouldn't. No, he thought, they should. They should kiss at least once a day for the rest of their natural lives.

They should raise a half-dozen kids, some cattle and a few horses on this piece of land.

But once again, he knew better than to voice that thought. He would keep it to himself, maybe replacing that nightmare with this dream.

"I need to get ready," she whispered.

"I know."

She rested her forehead against his chest. He hugged her close, making the moment last as long as possible. When she stepped away, his arms felt empty. He knew that someday they would work this out. He would find a way to make her his.

As if she knew what he was thinking, she said, "Duke, this isn't real. It's you learning you have a daughter and me acting a little bit vulnerable."

He let her go without telling her she was dead wrong. It wasn't only about Lilly. It was about something he'd never felt before. He wasn't a green kid who mistook his feelings for her. This was the most real relationship he'd ever experienced.

A man didn't walk away from that.

Oregon drove home from Austin in a daze. She didn't know what to think or how to feel.

She didn't know how to go home and face Lilly. Or Duke.

She drove down the dirt road and rather than going all the way to the end, she stopped at Breezy's. Jake, who was climbing into his truck, waved. She waved back, as if everything would be okay. And it would, she told herself. She'd been repeating that over and over on the way home. God hadn't gotten her this far to forget her.

Breezy walked out the front door, a twin on each hip. Breezy had taken to motherhood, and to life in Martin's Crossing.

"You're home," Breezy said, easing the twins down to stand on the porch.

"Was Duke wondering if I wouldn't come back?"

"Not at all. He did want me to tell you, if I saw you, that he and Lilly are in town. His evening shift cook didn't come in, so he's stuck at the diner till closing time."

"I should probably go pick up Lilly." Oregon turned to go, but Breezy stopped her.

"She was running the cash register and having the time of her life, last I heard. And I'm going to go out on a limb and say that maybe you need some girl time."

"I'm good." But as she said it she could feel

the sting of tears in her eyes, feel her throat tighten.

"Are you?" Breezy asked.

"Yes, of course." But a tear trickled down her cheek.

"Right, so why don't you come in, and we'll discuss how great you are over tea. Or coffee."

"Coffee would be nice."

They sat on the patio, watching the twins playing on a plastic slide in the backyard. The dog Daisy curled up nearby as if to guard the two little girls. Breezy watched them with a sweet look of contentment. Oregon wanted that. She wanted not to face battles. She wanted life to ease into a simple rhythm with no surprises.

"I have tiny squash in my garden." Breezy broke into the silence with conversation that had nothing to do with Oregon. It was a relief.

"I started a container garden at the shop," Oregon admitted. "And I've already killed it."

"Don't worry. I'll have plenty to share. Duke makes a great stir-fry. A man who can break a horse, fix a fence and cook." Breezy shot her a sly look. "What a catch."

"I'm not interested in catching anything."

"Violet, give Rosie a turn," Breezy called

out to the girls then settled a steady look on Oregon. "Right. Of course not."

"Breezy, that isn't why I'm here. I didn't come to Martin's Crossing because I felt some need to force Duke into marrying the mother of his child. I came here for Lilly, because she deserves a father. She deserves to have someone there for her. I mean, what if something happened to me?"

That was when she lost it. The dam broke, and the tears poured. Breezy immediately hugged her tight.

"Oregon, you've got to tell me what's going on."

Oregon shook her head. She pulled away from Breezy, wiping at her eyes. She watched the twins play, and she felt a longing so deep that it ached inside her. Breezy's hand was on her arm.

"I'm okay." Oregon repeated the mantra she'd been telling herself for almost two years now. Sometimes the fear crept in on her, but for the most part, she believed that she was okay.

"Because people who are okay always burst into tears at the drop of a hat."

"Hormones," Oregon admitted. That much was the truth.

Breezy sat there, watching her, watching the twins with one eye. "It's more than hormones."

Oregon sighed, wiping the last tears that trickled down her cheeks. "Eighteen months ago I was diagnosed with endometrial cancer. They caught it early and did a full hysterectomy."

Breezy's hand clutched hers. "I'm so sorry."

Oregon nodded and drew in a breath. "Me, too."

"That's why you came here?"

"Yes. It made me realize what a fragile thing life can be. And I wouldn't want Lilly left alone. I wouldn't want her left in the care of my mother. I want her to have stability and roots, not the constant drifting I endured as a kid. I definitely wanted more for my daughter."

"But you're okay now?" Breezy asked, giving Oregon's hand a squeeze.

"I think so. I haven't felt great lately, and decided to get it checked. They're going to run tests next week. It's probably nothing."

"I'm sure it's nothing." Breezy sounded so sure. Oregon felt a surge of relief, and faith. It felt good to tell someone.

"I'm sure it is, too."

"You can't go alone. I'll go with you. Or Duke can go, and Lilly can stay with me."

"I'm not going to tell Duke."

Breezy's eyes widened. "Why not?"

"Because I don't want to give him any more reasons to take care of me. He does like to take over." Her heart, her life, her peace of mind, those were the things he was taking control of. And it scared her.

"Why in the world wouldn't you want Duke to help you?"

For a minute she observed the twins at play. They were about to pounce on the Border collie, but the dog caught on and moved. The twins gave up and went back to the slide, having a brief fight over who would go first.

Why wouldn't she want Duke to help her? She knew the answer to that question. Because she was this close to falling in love with him. Because he was strong and caring, because he made her believe that a man might stay forever.

When had a man ever stayed in her life? The answer was never.

Chapter Eleven

Oregon drove to church on Sunday morning glad that the week was over. Not that it had been a bad week. But she needed Sunday. She needed church, needed a moment to slow down and sit in God's presence. In the seat next to her, Lilly was talking about her horse and going over her "things to do when the cast is off" list. Normal. Oregon felt the tension of the week draining away.

"Mom, do you think you and Duke will get married?"

Oregon nearly slammed on the brakes. Somehow she kept a steady foot on the gas. "I'm sorry, what?"

"You heard me. Don't act like you didn't."

A phrase Oregon had used more than once on her daughter was suddenly being used on her. "All right, I did hear you, but I can't believe what I'm hearing."

"I don't think it's such a crazy idea," Lilly said, as if it made more sense than chocolate on a bad day. And Oregon could have really used some chocolate right about then.

"You think not?"

"Well, the two of you have a daughter. In case you missed it, that would be me."

Oregon laughed. "No, I haven't missed that part of the equation. But you have to understand that Duke and I aren't... We weren't..." She sighed. "Duke and I were never a couple. It was..."

There was no explanation that made sense. She glanced at Lilly to check her reaction. Lilly continued to stare her down. Oregon drove into the church parking lot, thankful she had a reprieve. Even if it didn't last long.

"Mom, I get it. I'm not a kid."

Oregon arched a brow at that but didn't say anything. She didn't have to. Lilly wrinkled her nose.

"Okay, sure, I'm a kid. But I know what happened. I'm just saying that now...well, the two of you seem to like each other. Or at least you like to kiss."

"You are a kid. And no, we don't." She bit

her bottom lip and peeked at her daughter, because the last statement wasn't necessarily true. Being kissed by Duke Martin might just be at the top of her "best things ever" list.

"Yeah, you do," Lilly said with firm conviction. "I've seen you. It's kind of gross, but I'm okay with you liking each other."

"Gee, thanks."

Lilly smirked. "It will help when you get married."

Oregon groaned as she pulled into a parking space. "We're *not* getting married. That isn't why we're here, Lilly. I brought you here because I wanted you to have a dad."

"Yeah, I know. And Mom, I'm sorry that you don't know your dad. I wish you did. And I hope if he's out there somewhere, he's as great as mine."

"Thank you, honey. But I think I'm long past wishing for my father. I have you, and that's the best thing ever."

Lilly opened the car door. "Yeah, I am great. I'm just saying, if you and Duke decide to get married, I'm okay with that."

"We're not getting married," she called out as Lilly hurried away on her crutches. "And slow down, you'll break your other leg."

"Who are you not marrying?"

At the deep voice, she froze. Slowly she turned to face Duke. She felt heat settle in her cheeks as she looked at him. Her gaze lingered because today, in dark jeans, cowboy boots and a dark gray button-down shirt, he looked maddeningly good. He acted as if he knew her thoughts, and something inside her eased. She hadn't seen him for a couple of days, and she'd missed him.

If she had to be honest, she liked more than his kisses. She liked Duke. She liked the way he made her smile when she didn't want to. And how he made her feel like trusting someone wouldn't be so awful.

"No one," she whispered, grimacing as she said it, because they both knew it wasn't the truth.

"I see. You're marrying no one. But our daughter would like for you to marry someone."

"She's twelve, Duke. She has ideas about family, about you and me."

"You don't have to explain. I have ideas about family and you and me, too."

Oh, her heart wanted to believe that. She wanted to believe in marriage that lasted, with someone who didn't walk out.

"We should go inside now." She was feeling

cowardly and didn't want to put everything on the line. All of her baggage, the cancer, the hysterectomy. It was a lot of baggage.

"Right, the bell is ringing." He took her hand, and together they walked up the steps.

Inside the church they found Lilly in a pew midway down, seated next to Brody. Lilly laughed at something he said.

"I don't trust those two," Duke said, mirroring the words she'd been thinking.

"Neither do I."

They took a seat in the pew behind them. Oregon leaned forward to tell her daughter to hush. Then the service started. The music brought her the peace she'd been looking for. The words of the hymns even spoke of that peace. She closed her eyes and let go of the fear, the doubt.

God hadn't brought her this far to forget her. She knew that.

After the service was over, people in the sanctuary gathered in small groups, talking, making lunch plans. Oregon spotted Nedine threading her way through the crowd. The woman was dressed in a colorful caftan and bright red cowboy boots. She'd tied her long hair back with a scarf.

"Just the person I've been wanting to talk to," Nedine said when she got to Oregon.

"Oh, okay."

Ned hugged her. "Don't be afraid, I'm not going to ask for too much."

"I'm not afraid. Much."

Ned laughed. "It's just that I have these kittens."

"No!"

"Now, now, hear me out. I won't ask you to take them all. But I have two of the cutest little males in the world. They're out of my Manx momma cat and who knows what tomcat. But they have bobbed tails. One is orange, and the other is a tabby. They won't mind being outside since you have that nice barn back behind your place."

"Did Lilly put you up to this? She just got some crazy big bird that yells things like 'Fire' in the middle of the night."

Ned hooted at that. "Oh, that's perfect. And I'm just teasing, I don't have any cats. I'm allergic. I heard about the bird, and Lilly and I thought it might be fun to ask you about kittens. She said you really don't like cats."

"I don't mind them. As long as they belong to someone else." Oregon laughed. "You really had me going."

"Oh, if you could have seen the look on your face. But I tell you what, I'd love to take Lilly home with me for the day. My niece, Julia, is here visiting for a few days, and I thought the girls might like to go fishing."

Lilly approached them, a girl with light brown hair and big dimples at her side. "Can I go, Mom?"

Oregon nodded. "You can go. I'll pick you up this afternoon."

"Could she spend the night?" Julia asked, looking from Ned to Oregon.

Ned shrugged. "I really don't mind. I've got the day off tomorrow. We might build a fire in the fire pit and roast marshmallows."

"I think that would be fine." Lilly gave her a hug that nearly knocked her off her feet. "But you'll need clothes."

"I'll swing past your place on my way home," Ned offered. "And tomorrow after they wake up, I'll drive her home."

With all of the details taken care of, Oregon gathered up her things. When she straightened, Joe appeared at her side, a little wan and not his normal jovial self. "Joe, I haven't seen you in days."

He kept his hat in his hands and studied her. She thought he looked sad. Regretful. It was an odd mix of emotions to see on his normally smiling face.

"It has been a few days. I wanted to check on Lilly. I can see she's doing well. And how are you holding up?"

"I'm good, Joe. Thank you." She rested a hand on his arm. "Are you okay?"

"Of course I am. I've been a little under the weather, but nothing serious. How is Lilly doing? Is she adjusting?"

She didn't know what to say. She knew he had to mean about Duke being Lilly's father.

Joe cleared his throat. "He's a good man, and I imagine he'll be a good dad to her. Some men are just natural-born fathers."

"Yes, I guess some are." She didn't understand the direction of this conversation.

At the front of the church she saw Duke talking to Boone Wilder. The younger man was showing him a folder. Duke nodded and glanced their way. Her heart gave a heavy thud because the look on his face couldn't be called gentle at that moment.

Joe saw it, too. "It seems as if he's gotten some bad news."

"Yes, it appears that way." She clutched her purse and her bible. "Joe, if you need anything at all, please call me."

"I will. And thank you, Oregon." He walked away, shuffling his feet a bit. She had never seen Joe shuffle. He seemed to have aged ten years in the past week.

Oregon headed for the front door, thinking she would bypass Duke and more difficult conversations. Of course he followed her out the door, catching up with her on the sidewalk.

"Where's Lilly?" he asked as he strode next to her.

"Going home with Ned for the night. Lilly is going to spend time with her niece, Julia."

"Then maybe we could spend some time together."

Oregon stopped at her car. "What were you and Boone discussing?"

"Business." He smiled as he said it. "We could roast hot dogs on a fire and maybe watch the moon come up together."

"You and Boone?"

"Yes, because I love moonlit walks with Boone Wilder." He gave an exaggerated shudder. "Oregon, you know we need to talk."

"Why do we need to talk?"

"You've hardly said a word to me all week. You've been quiet and pale, and I'm worried." He reached for her hand, but his fingers just grazed hers before moving away. "More than anything, I'd really like to spend some time with you. Alone."

She arched a brow at him, and he laughed. "Too much?" he asked.

"A little over the top. Okay, we can talk. I'm going to go home and get a few things done. Maybe five o'clock."

"Five o'clock is good. Jake asked me to help him doctor some sick calves."

She nodded and reached for her car door. Duke got there first. He opened the door and waited as she slid behind the wheel. When she looked up, he had a strange expression on his face, as if he was inspecting her. She told herself that Breezy hadn't told him.

Of course Breezy wouldn't tell.

Duke rode his ATV down to Oregon's at five that afternoon. It was hot, and the breeze from the open vehicle felt pretty good. He parked the four-wheeler next to her car and climbed off, smoothing down his still-damp hair. As he walked around to the back of the house, Oregon stepped out the back door, baking sheet in her hands as she headed for the grill. He met her and lifted the lid.

"We were just going to grill hot dogs on a bonfire," he said.

"I thought vegetables would help me feel like I was eating something with more nutritional value so I made kebabs." She looked up at him. "Sometimes I am my mother's daughter."

"There's nothing wrong with eating vegetables." He took the pack off his back. "I have everything in here. Including the slightly squished buns."

She took the backpack and led him inside where she had already made tea. It was sitting on the counter, the glass pitcher damp from condensation. "It's really too warm to start a fire."

"I know." He stood there in the familiar kitchen and studied the face of a woman he had known for a little over a year. In the past couple of weeks she'd gone from the woman he rarely spoke to, to the woman he shared a child with.

It changed things inside him. It made him look at her from a different perspective. She'd given him a child. Man, that was huge.

Especially when, not even a month ago, he hadn't wanted kids of his own. He hadn't thought about settling down or having a family. No, he'd wanted to avoid those two things at all costs.

But here he was, and here she was. As much as he hadn't wanted to be this involved in someone else's life, he was. They were connected by a horse-crazy girl and a ton of emotions. He watched her, noticing shadows in her eyes and worry she couldn't hide.

"Tell me what's going on," he said, wrapping one arm around her waist and pulling her close.

"Nothing is going on." She reached for the tea. "If you get ice I'll pour us a glass."

"All right. On one condition. We have our tea, and you tell me why you have dark circles under your eyes. And don't tell me it isn't any of my business. You're the mother of my daughter. You are my business."

She looked up at him, her eyes narrowing. "Really? You're in charge of me now?"

"No, but I care."

She let out a breath, and her gaze dropped to the floor. "Duke, let's not go there."

"I'm not sure where we're going, Oregon. But I do know that you need to talk to me. I'm not crazy about surprises."

For a minute she studied the view out the window, then nodded. "Okay."

It didn't feel like he'd won any sort of victory. He got the ice, and she poured tea. It was hot outside so they sat at the kitchen table. He took the chair across the table from her. The table was small; their feet touched underneath. She kept her eyes on the glass she held between her hands.

"This isn't a quick story."

He nodded once. "I didn't think it would be. But I have a feeling I'm about to find out why you came to Martin's Crossing."

"You are." She took a drink of tea, a long, slow sip. He watched her throat move as she swallowed. Her eyes closed briefly, and her dark lashes brushed pale skin. When she looked back at him, he almost lost it. He wanted to pull her close and tell her he'd fix everything.

He'd never wanted this, a woman to be responsible for, to make sure she had everything she needed. But here he was, and there she was. And he knew he'd walk on hot coals for her or for Lilly.

"About eighteen months ago, I was diagnosed with endometrial cancer. They caught it early, and they did a hysterectomy." She blinked a few times. "They contained the cancer, and I've been cancer-free ever since. But it made me think about mortality, and it also made me realize that Lilly needs some-one else. In case…"

In case anything should happen to her.

He wanted to tell her nothing would. He wanted to promise her that he'd protect her. He'd keep her healthy. But he knew that no one could make those promises.

He'd made promises like that too many times in the field. He'd promised men that they'd be okay. That they would go home to their families. All of those empty promises rushed back to him now, taunting him.

Her hands covered his. "Duke, don't. I'm not asking you to make me promises. I trust God. I'm not going to stop trusting."

What did he say to that? Because he hadn't ever been the guy with faith overflowing. He'd been the guy who went to church when Jake dragged him. He'd said some prayers for men, begging God to keep them alive. And now, in just the past few weeks, he'd started to find a faith that felt a little different, a little more real.

What he didn't want was for this woman to be in his life only temporarily. As he sat there looking at her, head bent, hands still clasped over his, he got the feeling that God was telling him to trust. No matter what the outcome. Even if things didn't turn out the way he wanted. He had to trust.

In Afghanistan he'd made promises he'd had no right making. He'd wanted to make those men feel safe and give them hope. All too often he'd known they didn't believe his promises. But he had believed. And then he'd lost faith.

He took a deep breath, and it shuddered in his chest. "What's changed, Oregon? You said they got it all, but you came here because it made you aware that something could happen. That doesn't explain what is happening now."

"I went to the doctor last week. They want to run some tests. I've scheduled the appointment for Wednesday when I go to Austin for Lilly's appointment."

"And you were going to, what? Go through this alone?"

"I went through it alone the last time."

"That wasn't on my watch."

A slow flicker of a smile touched her lips. "You tend to take over."

"Yeah, it's a habit."

"I'm used to taking care of myself."

"That's a bad habit, too," he chided.

He had a feeling it was more that she didn't trust anyone else to take care of her. He got that. But he wasn't going to argue with her. He wouldn't be that person in her life. He'd never let her down or walk away. But words weren't going to prove anything to Oregon Jeffries.

Because he'd spent a lifetime listening to broken promises, he got that. He'd had a father that wouldn't stop drinking. He'd been told that his mother would come back. He knew that words were just words.

"What can I do?"

She looked him straight in the eyes as she held tight to his fingers across the table. "Hold me. Because I'm so tired. I'm tired of worrying. Tired of feeling like I'm not a whole person."

It didn't take more than that to move him to her side. She stood, and he pulled her close, sliding fingers through hair that felt like silk. He brushed a light kiss against her lips before claiming her in a kiss that he hoped would show her she was still a woman. And it would take a man stronger than him to resist her.

Chapter Twelve

Duke took Monday off. He'd have preferred taking the whole week off and maybe finding a beach on a desert island. Since that obviously couldn't happen, he sat on the deck of the diner with a cup of coffee watching the street for Boone Wilder. When he saw the old truck with the big tires turn down Main Street, he stood up and walked down the steps. Boone got out, touching the brim of his cowboy hat as he rounded to the passenger side to open the door.

The young woman getting out looked like he expected her to look. She was pretty, from money and nervous. She brushed her dark hair back from her face and surveyed the street with the few businesses and a handful of cars and trucks. Typical slow Monday in Martin's Crossing.

He waited for them, coffee in hand. He took a sip and leaned against the post. Boone spoke to the young woman, nodded toward Oregon's All Things and then he pointed to the No Bar and Grill.

Boone led her up the steps. She wore a floral dress with a jean jacket and high heels. Her cologne was sweet and young. He hoped Boone knew how to mind his manners.

"Duke Martin, this is Sissy Andrews. She's from Dallas."

"Sissy, nice to meet you." She took his hand in a brief handshake.

"Nice to meet you. I take it you know where my father is."

"Yes, we do." He showed her the picture. "You're sure this is your dad?"

"Of course. Is he sober?"

"Been sober every day I've known him. Why isn't there a missing person's report?"

"Because we wanted to keep it quiet. If customers knew that he had taken off, they would doubt if their orders were going to be filled and projects finished. We've hired investigators. They traced him to a hospital in Austin, and then he disappeared again. That's when we contacted the police for help."

"He hasn't contacted you in over six months?"

"A few letters. A phone call once in a while. Does he have a home here?"

"He does now. For a while he slept in the Christmas nativity."

She shook her head. "He really is sane. He's a great businessman. He's been sober for fifteen years except a relapse after my mom died. I was afraid that maybe he'd slipped."

"Not that I know of." Duke turned as another car pulled in. "There he is now."

Joe got out of his old car. He stopped, stared up at the diner, at Duke, and then fixed his gaze on the young woman standing next to Duke. Joe shook his head, and even from that distance Duke saw him sigh. With slow, steady steps, he started down the sidewalk toward the diner.

"Why did he come here?" Sissy Andrews asked in a voice that wavered.

"I think you'll have to ask him." Duke took a step away from her. He held out a hand to Joe as he climbed the stairs. Joe took the hand, shook it, and then he turned to Sissy.

"I see you found me." He looked at Duke. "Or did you do this?"

"I did it, Joe. I had to know who you are and why you're here."

Joe shook his head. "Being a dad changes

a man. It makes him think a little more about who is in his life."

"Yes, or in his daughter's life." Duke patted Joe on the back. "She's been worried about you."

"I know, and I'm sorry."

"Were you drinking?" Sissy asked, her voice trembling just a little.

Joe walked over to a table and sat down. He pushed out a chair for his daughter, and she took it. "Dad?"

"Yes, I was drinking. But I haven't had a drink in a while. I left because I had things I couldn't ignore. I knew that Morgan would hold down the fort. I knew you'd be there to make sure he did. But I had to put some things to rest and make amends. I got sober, and I came here to finish the rest of my program."

"Dad, why here?" She reached for his hand. "You slept in a nativity?"

He grinned at that. "It was good enough for our savior."

"Yes, but you're a little older than he was at the time, and Texas is a little colder than Bethlehem."

"It wasn't so bad. And I didn't stay there long. It was just, I don't know, something I needed to do. If the press heard about it, they'd think I was off my rocker and the business would suffer."

"No one is going to know. But now is the time for honesty."

Joe sighed. He brushed a hand over his haggard face, covered with gray whiskers. "Yes, time for honesty. But for that honesty, you have to come with me. I have someone I want you to meet."

"Mom has only been gone..."

He cut her off, kissing her cheek as he stood. "This isn't about replacing your mother. Yes, she's been gone three years. But she was the love of my life. She looked at an old drunk, and she saw someone worth loving. Losing her, well, it almost did me in. But I still have you."

As the older man walked down the steps, his daughter at his side, Duke knew where he would go. He knew the lives he would change. Hopefully the changes would be good.

As they crossed the street to Oregon's, Lilly came out of the shop. She waited on the sidewalk for them, a big smile on her face. When Joe reached her, he smoothed her dark hair and gave her a hug.

"You know, I think you're about the best

thing ever," the older man said. "Where are you off to?"

Lilly beamed at the older man. "I'm going to the park to hang out with friends. I can at least swing."

"Well, you have a good time and be careful."

"I will. Later, Joe." Lilly's gaze landed on Sissy, openly curious before she turned to leave them. "See ya."

Joe watched her go, and then he took a deep breath and faced Duke.

"Well, this is it. I don't know why I waited so long," Joe said as he opened the door to Oregon's. "Foolish. That's all I can say."

"Dad, what do you mean?" Sissy followed him inside. "Why are we here?"

The bell over the door chimed. Oregon came out of the back of the shop. She looked from Joe to Sissy, her gaze cautious. Duke wondered if she would thank him, or never talk to him again for interfering.

"Good morning, everyone." Oregon frowned a little as she glanced Duke's direction. "Is something wrong?"

"Can we put up the Closed sign for a few minutes?" Duke asked, turning to switch the sign before she answered.

"Sure, since you already are."

"Oregon, we need to talk." Joe took her by the arm. "Do you still have furniture in the back?"

"Yes, of course." She pulled away from him, her attention focusing on the other woman at Joe's side. "Are you a friend of Joe's?"

"I'm his daughter, Sissy Andrews." Sissy held out a hand to Oregon. He wondered if they saw what he could so easily see. He didn't think so. They were too busy being wary to notice the similarities.

"Nice to meet you." Oregon's tone brightened, and suspicion slipped away. "We all love Joe so much."

They walked into the living area of the shop. Oregon pointed to the sofa. She sat on a stool. Duke came to stand behind her, resting a hand on her shoulder. Looking at him, he saw her expression change.

"What's going on?"

Oregon sat on the stool, willing her body not to tremble. She wouldn't jump to conclusions. It wouldn't do her any good. She waited, almost calmly, Duke's hand on her shoulder. She placed her hand over his, holding it there.

"Joe?" Duke pushed again.

"This isn't easy," he said.

"Joe, you're making me nervous." Oregon looked from Joe to the woman, Sissy. She appeared to be in her midtwenties and obviously wasn't impoverished.

Did this mean he wasn't the homeless man they'd all believed?

"A long time ago," Joe began, "a kid from Dallas had a wealthy family with several profitable businesses. And he spent a lot of time drinking. He met a woman and they eloped. His family wasn't happy, but he thought she'd make everything right for him, like she could fix him."

Oregon opened her mouth but Joe stopped her.

"Let me finish before I lose my courage. They had a daughter. Even that didn't stop him. He continued to drink and sometimes he wasn't the nicest guy in the world. Eventually his wife asked for a divorce. He gave it to her, knowing he'd never see his daughter again."

Everything blurred. Oregon shook her head. "Joe." It came out as a sob.

"I'm so sorry, peaches." He got up and started toward her. She held up a hand. He stopped.

"No, sit down." Her voice shook, and she

was suddenly chilled. She moved, dislodging the comfort of Duke's hand. Too much comfort and she'd fall apart. Right now she had to hold on to whatever anger she could in order to keep from crying.

"Why?" She blinked away the tears that threatened to fall.

"I thought you'd be better off without me. I wasn't a father. I was a drunk, and I wasn't always a nice drunk."

"You could have gotten help."

"I know that. There are a lot of things I know now. I know that I should have gotten help. I know that I should have kept in contact and made an effort to be in your life. But I also knew your mom would keep you safe, and you'd have a good life."

She hopped down off the stool. "A good life? My mother has been married a half-dozen times. Until I was fourteen, she tried to tell me I had to call each one of them Daddy. But they weren't, were they? And I knew that. I knew that there had been someone, and he had loved me. And then he'd disappeared. I moved more than a dozen times before I turned eighteen. Every time I would get settled and think that maybe, just maybe, this time we would stay somewhere, she'd decide to move again. You were both selfish, and I was the one who paid the price for that selfishness."

Joe's face crumpled in regret, and tears filled his eyes.

"You're right. I can't deny that we were selfish, and you were the victim. I can only ask you to forgive me and hope we can build a relationship. I hope you'll let me be a father to you, a grandfather to Lilly."

That meant telling Lilly. Oregon stood at the door, thinking about how she would do that. "How am I supposed to tell my daughter that her friend Joe is her grandfather?"

"We'll do it together." Duke was at her side, his hand on her back. "Your biggest problem is that you act like you have to tackle everything alone. Maybe that's how you've survived for thirty years. Now might be the time to let other people help you. Including the father of that little girl you're so worried about."

She closed her eyes and tried to regroup, to find the strength she'd always relied on to get her through. Duke was right, she wasn't good at letting other people in, letting them help. No one had ever been in her life long enough to be trusted that way. She hadn't been able to count on her mother to be there for her. But Lilly didn't have to live like that. Lilly had parents who would make sure she was taken care of.

"Maybe I shouldn't be here." Sissy stood up, her hands clasped in front of her. Her dark gray eyes were filled with tears. They shared a similar heartache. Different, but similar. Oregon took a long look at the younger woman. Her sister. She saw pieces of herself in Sissy Andrews. In her dark gray eyes, in the shape of her face. They were sisters. It unsettled Oregon but it also forced her to the other woman's side.

"I'm so sorry," Oregon told Sissy as she took her in a tight hug. "I am so very sorry that you've been hurt by this."

"Me?" Sissy pulled back. "I can't even imagine how you feel."

"We have a lot of time to make up for." Oregon hugged her once more. "And I have to find the best way to tell Lilly."

"We should tell her together," Joe said in a gentle voice. A voice full of regret.

"There is so much I need to tell her. I don't know where to start." She reached for the door. How had life gotten so complicated? "I need to think."

Joe stood, as if to follow. "Oregon, I've hurt you. I know that. But I love you. I love Lilly.

I've stayed here in order to build a relationship with the two of you. I should have found a way to tell you sooner, but it wasn't as easy as I thought."

Oregon saw the similarities. Because she had waited almost a year to tell Duke that he was Lilly's father. She made eye contact with him, and he offered a grim smile.

"Joe, I do understand that it wasn't easy. I just, it's been almost thirty years."

"Twenty-eight years and three months," Joe said without a trace of humor. "And I've regretted every year, every month, every day."

"We all have regrets," Oregon said, then she pushed the door open. "I have to go."

"Can I see her?" Joe asked as she headed out the door.

"Yes, Joe, you can see her. But not today. I can't do this today."

As she walked down the sidewalk, Oregon realized she had company. She glanced back over her shoulder at Duke. Of course. She kept walking, but he caught up to her.

"You did this?" she asked.

"Yeah, I did this. I guess it's the fatherhood thing. I started to worry about Joe being around my daughter. I haven't cared too much about his identity. He didn't bother anyone and didn't seem to be a danger, so why push it? But I didn't want to take a chance with your or Lilly's safety. So I had the guys do some checking."

"I wish you hadn't."

"Oregon, he's your father. He was going to tell you eventually. He wanted to be involved in your life. My guess is, Joe was the one who has been helping people in town."

She stopped walking. "He bought the building and deeded it to me."

Someone had bought her building in December, and it had been deeded over to her with the insurance and taxes all paid. Of course people in town had wondered if it was Joe, or even Breezy with her newly inherited money. But now she knew. It had been her father. Joe.

"He wanted to take care of you." Duke reached for her hand. "It's what a father does."

"Well he's a little too late for that."

"I don't think so. I think he's here just in time."

Her throat tightened. She pinched the bridge of her nose. "Don't, Duke. Don't make me cry. Not today. Why are you following me?"

He tugged on her hand and stopped her. "You don't know why I'm following you?"

She shook her head, and she saw that he looked hurt. She didn't want to hurt him.

"I'm following you because this isn't about you. It isn't about Lilly. It's about us. This will change her life, your life, and that means it changes my life. I'm going because a dad should be involved in a conversation that is life changing. You see, Oregon, some dads want to be there for their kids."

She flattened her palm against his cheek. "I'm sorry, and you're right. I'm glad she has you."

"You both have me."

She moved her hand from his cheek and shook her head. "No, Duke. She has you."

"You can both have me."

She started walking, but he remained at her side.

"Oregon?"

She didn't slow down. "Don't. This isn't fair. You can rescue Lilly, but you can't rescue me."

"What if I want to marry you, not rescue you?"

At that she came to a quick stop on the sidewalk. She looked up, frowning just a little. "That isn't a relationship. You want to be there for Lilly, and I wouldn't want it any other way.

But I can't let you marry me out of some sense of responsibility."

"Lady, you are so wrong. But I'm not going to argue right now. I am going to tell you this. The one thing you can't argue with is that we make pretty decent parents. And you can't deny that everything else between us is pretty amazing, too."

She couldn't deny it, so she changed the subject. "I have to think. I need to tell Lilly about Joe. I also need to tell her the truth about my health."

"Let's wait until the morning. We can have a night to sleep on it and pray on it."

"Okay, I can do that. We'll tell Joe that we'll all sit down together tomorrow and tell her."

Somehow Oregon found herself on the deck of Duke's No Bar and Grill. Across the street she had a father and a sister. Down the block at the park her daughter was playing with friends, not knowing that her life was about to take a drastic turn. Not for the worse, though. She refused to believe this would be for the worse.

Hadn't she wanted Lilly to have family? A safety net. And now she had one. The strongest part of that net was sitting across from Oregon. And he thought they should get married.

She sighed.

"You okay?" Duke asked.

"Yes, I'm good. Shocked, but good."

"Really? Because I don't think you should be okay. I think you should be angry, hurt and I don't know what else."

She leaned back in the chair. "What good would all that do? My mom has managed to leave a trail of destruction behind her. And she doesn't think so. She has always convinced herself that she's doing the right thing, the fun thing or the adventurous thing. All of these years I've asked her to tell me who my dad is, and she's acted like it was impossible to tell, and yet here he was the whole time."

"What did you tell Lilly about her father?"

She brushed a hand across her face. "I told her she wasn't a mistake. She is the best thing that has ever happened to me. I told her I would find her father for her. And I did. Maybe I took too long, or didn't tell you soon enough, but I brought her here."

"Would you have brought her if…"

She knew he didn't want to say the word. She said it for him. "If it hadn't been for the cancer? Yes, I would have."

"Thank you. And for the record, you can

reject me all you want, but I'm here for you. Even when you say you don't need me."

The words filled an empty space in her heart. It would have been easy to step into his embrace, to accept the comfort he obviously wanted to give. But she couldn't.

It wasn't fair to expect him to be that person. Yes, they had a common bond, their daughter. But they'd only had one night years ago. That didn't make her his problem.

A selfish part of her was thankful that he cared, though. Another part of her, a big part, wanted to be his problem to care about.

"We should go back to the shop. It wasn't right to walk away. I just needed a few minutes to think."

"And now?"

"I think we all sit down with Lilly. Tomorrow. Is that okay?" she asked, knowing it was not just her decision to make.

"I think it's okay."

As they walked back to her shop, she thought about how great it would feel to have a right to the man at her side. If they were married, if she accepted his proposal, they would have each other. He would be there for Lilly, and for her.

But then she remembered what he'd said

days ago. That he'd like to have a half-dozen kids if they were all like Lilly.

Duke could give her everything. But she could never give him those children. It didn't seem like a fair trade.

Chapter Thirteen

Oregon woke up late the next morning. When she got to the kitchen to make coffee, she found a pot already brewing. Not only was the coffee already being made, there were muffins on the counter, too. She walked to the window and looked out. Duke was heading toward the house from the barn, his white cowboy hat pulled low to block the morning sun. Lilly walked next to him. He said something, pushing his hat back a bit as he leaned to Lilly's level. She laughed. They stopped to look out at the field. They were probably discussing her horse and the walking cast she hoped to get the next afternoon.

Footsteps behind her meant she wasn't alone.

She turned, smiling at Sissy. She had stayed

the night with them because Joe didn't have an extra bed in his small apartment. Sissy had slept in Lilly's bed, and Lilly had stayed with Duke. Oregon and her sister had stayed up late into the night sharing stories of very different childhoods.

Sissy had lived a privileged life with parents who adored her. Joe had sometimes struggled with his alcoholism but had worked hard at staying sober. He'd been sober for fifteen years when Sissy's mom passed away, and he'd started to drink again. He'd hid it from everyone, still functioning and managing the business.

Oregon had talked about her own mother, a woman who flitted from relationship to relationship, reinventing herself each time.

"They seem close." Sissy nodded, indicating Duke and Lilly.

"Yes, they're getting closer every day," Oregon agreed as she watched Lilly and Duke. "I wasn't sure what would happen when I told her. Or him, for that matter."

Silence fell between them. Sissy eventually rested a hand on Oregon's arm.

"I hope you'll give our dad a chance," she said. "He's a good man. A little misguided at times, but he cares."

Oregon was sure Joe cared. "I think I'm more angry with my mother than with him. She didn't have to keep me from him."

"No, she didn't. He loved you. He has pictures from when you were little. I caught him looking at them once. He wouldn't tell me who you were, but he said something about how we were probably a lot alike."

"I want us to get to know each other. Lilly should have an aunt. And a grandfather." Isn't that what she'd prayed for? That her daughter would have family?

Duke and Lilly came through the door, laughing and joking. His gaze met Oregon's and she felt that look to the tips of her toes. It got a little harder to breathe with him in the same room. His presence made it hard to think, to remember why being together wasn't a good idea.

Sometimes she thought it might be. But what if they tried and couldn't make it work? She didn't want to do that to Lilly. She didn't want to do that to herself. It was one of the reasons she hadn't dated since giving birth to Lilly. Because she didn't want her daughter to have to deal with different men coming in and out of her life.

"I started coffee and brought muffins," he

said, reaching to ruffle their daughter's hair when she said something about him not baking the muffins, Ned did.

"Thank you." Oregon filled three cups with coffee. "I'm not really hungry."

"Eat," he ordered as he took his cup of coffee. He carried it to the table, along with two muffins in his left hand. He dropped one muffin on the table and tossed the other to Lilly, who had taken a seat.

Oregon grabbed a muffin and coffee. She motioned for Sissy to take the extra chair at the table. She wasn't in the mood to sit. Duke motioned for her to sit down, though. She shook her head.

"I really can't." She leaned against the counter.

"Why are you so nervous?" Lilly asked, after taking a bite of muffin. "And why is Joe coming out here? I thought we were going to close the store early today and go shopping."

"We have to talk." Oregon sipped her coffee, ignoring the continued looks her daughter gave her. "It's nothing."

"Let's eat so we can show Sissy that gelding of yours." Duke mentioned the horse, distracting Lilly. Oregon whispered a silent thank-you when he looked her way.

Lilly scarfed down the muffin in record time and grabbed her crutches. "Let's go."

"Give everyone a chance to finish their coffee," Oregon ordered.

Lilly groaned, but sat back down to wait impatiently for the adults who had the nerve to sip their coffee and talk. Every now and then Lilly groaned and Oregon would shoot her a warning look.

Duke drained the last of his coffee and stood, signaling an end to Lilly's torture.

Walking out to the barn together was a welcome distraction. Oregon walked behind Duke and Lilly, listening to the two of them talk and laugh about something that she couldn't hear. While she and Sissy waited at the fence, Duke and Lilly walked into the barn for a bucket of grain and a lead rope.

Duke called the horse up to the corral, shaking the bucket of grain. The gelding trotted up, slipping through the open gate that Duke closed behind him. The horse immediately shoved his nose into the bucket of grain, jerking his head up when the lead rope snapped onto his halter. Lilly waited by the corral fence for Duke to lead the horse over to where she stood.

Oregon and Sissy stood outside the corral.

Shoulder to shoulder, Oregon realized that she and the woman who was her sister were nearly the same height, and their hair was the same color. Standing there next to each other, it felt strangely right. She had a sister.

Growing up she'd had a few stepsisters and stepbrothers, but this sister was hers by blood. This sister couldn't be taken away.

"I'm glad we found each other," Oregon admitted, smiling at the woman standing next to her. "As complicated and strange as this has been, I'm glad."

"Me, too."

Joe pulled up in the old clunker car he'd been driving for a month or so. He got out, smiling when he saw the two of them together. As he walked up, Oregon saw it. She saw parts of herself in this man. She saw her chin, her eyes and her smile. She hadn't noticed that the twinkle in her daughter's eyes matched his.

"Good morning, girls." He kissed Sissy's cheek. He didn't move toward Oregon. He hesitated, as if waiting to see what their relationship would be.

She solved his dilemma by hugging him tight. "We are going to get through this, Joe."

"I'm glad, kiddo. I'm real glad to hear that." He turned his attention to the father and daughter in the corral. "Nice horse. She deserves that."

"She will earn that," Oregon insisted.

Joe nodded, chuckling just a little. "Of course."

"Hey, Joe!" Lilly finished feeding her horse and took the bucket away. The gelding nudged at shoulder, but Duke led the animal back out of the corral. "Mom told me you were going to be out today. How do you like my horse?"

"He's a nice-looking animal," Joe answered as Lilly came through the gate he'd opened for her.

"Thanks. I guess you're here to pick up Sissy?"

"I am, but we're not leaving yet." Joe gave her room to maneuver with the crutches. "I bet you're ready to ditch that cast."

She grimaced. "More than ready. I want to ride Chief, go swimming and scratch my foot!"

Oregon watched the two of them. Nothing had changed. They were still Lilly and Joe, two unlikely friends. She sighed, and when Duke reached for her hand, she laced her fingers through his.

"Let's go inside," Duke suggested to the group.

Lilly's eyes narrowed as she looked at him

but didn't say anything. Instead she walked through the front door that Joe had opened for her. Sissy followed, looking as hesitant as Oregon felt.

When Oregon walked into the room, Joe and Sissy were on the sofa. Lilly sat alone, worrying her bottom lip with her teeth. Oregon scooted her daughter over and sat next to her in the overstuffed chair she had plopped down in.

Duke grabbed a chair from the kitchen table and carried it back into the room. All the while they sat in silence. Oregon knew this wasn't the worst news she could give her daughter. It wasn't even bad news. It just felt huge, especially considering that within the past month Lilly had been in an accident, learned that Duke was her dad and now this.

Mothers were meant to protect children. Oregon had always kept Lilly safe. She'd tried to be the mom that her own mother had never managed to be. She'd held Lilly tight when Eugenia had recommended giving her up for adoption. Oregon had insisted she could raise her, and they'd be just fine. And they had been just fine. It hadn't been easy, but they'd survived. They would continue to survive.

"Okay, everyone stop staring and tell me

what's wrong." Lilly looked at them, swallowing loudly as her worried expression grew.

"Lilly, I'm not sure how to tell you…"

"Mom, just say it. I'm twelve and I think I can handle this."

"Okay. Lilly, just like you, I had a father. I didn't remember him, but I do remember that he loved me. And I always wanted to know him, to know who he was."

Lilly's gaze flew to Joe. "Are you my mom's dad?"

So much for Oregon's carefully planned speech about forgiving and accepting. She looked to Joe. Her dad.

He focused on Lilly. "I am, sweet pea. I came here because I wanted to make sure you were okay. That your mom was okay."

"You're my grandfather?" Lilly asked, coming out of the daze she'd been in. She shook her head a little.

"I'm your grandfather. Lilly, it's a long story, but my name is Joe Andrews. I have a manufacturing plant in Dallas. Sissy is my daughter from my second marriage. Your mother is my daughter from my first marriage. And you are definitely my granddaughter."

Lilly sat for a moment. "Wow, that's just crazy."

Joe chuckled. "Yes, it is."

"Why didn't my mom know you?" Lilly asked, full steam ahead as usual.

"Lilly," Oregon cautioned. "There are some things you don't need answers for, not right now."

"I'm twelve, not five."

Oregon looked to Joe and he nodded.

"I didn't know Joe because he had a problem with alcohol and my mother left him."

Lilly shook her head. "She should have told you."

Oregon agreed. "Yes, she should have. But she didn't. But Joe found us anyway, and I'm glad he did." She looked at the man who was her father and smiled. She was very glad he'd found her.

"So you'll stay here, though. Right?" Lilly asked.

"I'm going to have to go back to Dallas. I've left my business in the care of good managers and Sissy, but I can't leave it much longer. But I really want you all to visit. I'd actually love it if you could live there where we could get to know each other better. I know that's unfair of me, but you can't blame a man for trying."

"Joe, you have to understand, it's important that we stay here." Oregon took a deep breath, fortifying her resolve. She looked to Duke for encouragement. She'd prayed about this moment, about what to say and how.

"Of course you should stay here," Joe responded. "Dallas isn't that far away. I'll come visit every chance I get."

They talked a little while about their lives and Joe's home, about Sissy. Then the conversation died out.

"Oregon?" Duke prodded, his smile lending her strength.

She took a deep breath and nodded. She could do this. She had to do this today. She locked gazes with her daughter. She needed to do this while Lilly had family around her, so she would see that they had people who wouldn't leave them.

"Lilly, we have to talk about more than Joe. We have to talk about tomorrow."

It was a conversation no mother wanted to have with her child. Especially not her twelve-year-old daughter. She took a deep breath, felt the peace of knowing God was with her and that Duke would be there, too.

"Mom?" Lilly's eyes were wide and she reached for Oregon's hand.

"Give me a second."

With her family around her, Oregon finally told her daughter about the cancer. She explained that she'd been cancer-free and that the tests the next day were precautions. Everything would be fine, she promised, knowing that no one had guarantees.

"Of course you'll be okay, Mom," Lilly said with conviction. "And you should have told me a long time ago. I'm not a kid. I could have handled it."

"You are a kid. You're my kid. But you're right. I should have told you. This probably doesn't make sense, but I wanted to protect you." She wanted to make sure her daughter always felt safe and secure.

Lilly hugged her tight, as if she was the one who had to be strong. And that was the last thing Oregon wanted from her daughter. Growing up she'd been the strong one too many times for her mother. Eugenia had never seemed to worry, so Oregon had worried for them both. She had spent too much time worrying about where they would go next and what they would do when they got there.

She wanted more for Lilly than that.

Duke had watched his daughter handle everything that had been thrown at her. He'd expected to be the guy picking up pieces.

Instead, Lilly met everything head-on with maturity and faith that made him feel weak by comparison.

After lunch she'd insisted on taking Joe and Sissy outside to see everything. He guessed she might also be giving him time alone with her mom.

As he stood next to Oregon at the kitchen sink, he tried to brush aside Joe's offer to her, but he couldn't. Even though she had firmly rejected the idea of moving to Dallas, he thought about how that would change his life if she left.

True, he hadn't had a daughter very long. But she was his, and he didn't want to lose her. As he rinsed a plate, Oregon bumped her arm against his.

"I'm not going to take her away from you," she whispered close to his shoulder.

"I'd appreciate that."

"Then stop looking so worried." She kissed his shoulder. It unsettled him, that simple kiss.

"I'm not worried." He stacked the last plate in the drainer and looked at her. "Yeah, I'm worried. You've given me this amazing kid that I didn't even know I needed. But now I do need her. I don't want you to leave."

"We aren't leaving." Oregon rested her hand

on his arm. "I'm not going to do to her what my mom did to me, moving around so much. I'm glad I've found Joe and Sissy, but I don't have to live near them to build a relationship. Lilly has to be here with you."

"And what about you?" he couldn't help but ask. His phone rang. He looked at it and sighed. "Brody."

"Answer it. I wasn't going to answer your question anyway."

He couldn't let her get away with that.

"What you want matters too, you know."

"Answer the phone," she said, nudging him aside as she returned to the dishes.

Duke answered the phone. "What's up?"

"I need some help. We've got a hole in the fence down here on the road and about twenty head out."

"I'll be there in five." He tossed the towel on the counter and kissed Oregon's cheek. "Cattle out in the road."

"Go," she said.

"You know I'm not going to let you get away with not answering."

She nodded but shooed him away with her hands. Duke headed out the back door. Lilly was outside showing her newfound grandfather and aunt the flowers she'd planted.

"Where are you going?" she asked.

"To help Brody put some cattle in and fix a fence."

"Okay. Need some help?" she hurried along next to him, a pro on crutches these days.

A little of his tension melted away because his kid was like sunshine after a storm. "Thanks, but I think Brody and I can handle it."

"You'll come back?"

He climbed on the back of the ATV. "I'll be back."

When he pulled onto the main road, he saw Brody's truck parked half in the lane, half on the shoulder, the emergency flashers blinking. He hadn't exaggerated. Cattle were everywhere, and Brody was doing his best to keep them together. Daisy had followed Duke down the drive, running behind the four-wheeler. When she saw the cows, she went to work.

He pulled close with the four-wheeler. Brody moved to the other side of the herd while Daisy kept the cattle moving forward. When a cow with a calf tried to make an escape, Daisy circled wide and brought them back in. Before long they had the herd moving through the fence and back in the field.

Duke parked the ATV. Brody limped over

to where he'd stopped the vehicle. He nodded at the fence and posts that leaned in all directions.

"Looks like someone drove through it and then left it. Could have happened last night, and maybe the cattle just found it."

"Could be." Duke walked up to the fence. "Tire marks. Looks like someone got a little tangled up and had a hard time getting out."

"Yeah, probably kids." Brody practically hopped back to the four-wheeler and sat down on the seat. "It'll need to be fixed."

Duke headed for the truck and came back with pliers, wire cutters and a fence post hammer to pound loose posts back into the ground.

"You ever going to tell us what's going on with you?" Duke asked as he pulled on gloves. He shoved the tube of the fence post hammer over a metal post.

"You going to marry the mother of your daughter?" Brody hopped off the four-wheeler and hobbled over to help.

"I would if she…" At his brother's grin, Duke stopped. "We were talking about you."

He pounded the post back into the ground and went to the next.

"Yeah, I know, but did you see how I got you off the subject?" Brody shot him a grin as he pulled a strand of barbed wire. "Lilly's a great kid, and her mom is pretty easy on the eyes."

"And you can barely walk. I'm worried if you don't take care of this, you'll end up with permanent damage."

"Yeah, probably too late for that. Anyway, what's the deal with Joe and the woman that showed up yesterday? Someone said she's Joe's daughter."

"She is." Duke used pliers to tighten wire. "So is Oregon. That isn't common knowledge, so let's not make it town gossip."

Brody's eyes widened. "Wow. That's pretty huge. And don't worry, I'm not saying anything."

"Huge, yeah, I guess it is. He's Joe Andrews. He has a construction business and a manufacturing plant. Industrial heating systems of some type."

"Seriously? Why didn't anyone know that Joe Andrews was here?"

"Seriously. And they didn't call in the police. They didn't want customers to worry." Duke ran a hand over Daisy's head when she brushed against his leg. It felt good to talk. He'd been avoiding his family the past few days. He guessed they'd all avoided each other too much.

"You actually asked her to marry you?" Brody shook his head and laughed again. "Never thought you'd do something like that."

"Why?"

Brody shrugged. "Have you ever dated a woman longer than a month? I think most people would say the Martin men are afraid of commitment. At least until Jake met Breezy."

Afraid of commitment. Duke guessed he could agree. He hadn't ever thought of himself as afraid. More that he hadn't wanted to bother with something that seemed to cause more problems than it was worth. A kid changed everything.

He wanted Lilly to have more than he or Oregon had ever had. He wanted her to come home every day to two parents. He wanted her to go to sleep knowing they would both be there when she woke up. Yeah, he wanted stability for his kid, not for her to worry about parents not showing up for dinner.

He wanted Oregon to trust that he wouldn't walk out on them. And he wanted her to trust that he needed only her, not the things she couldn't give that she thought he might want later.

Like more children. He shook his head at the conversation he was having with himself. When he chanced a look at Brody, his younger brother grinned.

"My, how life gets complicated."

"Complicated doesn't begin to define this." Duke finished tightening the fence. "Go on up to the house. Make a doctor's appointment. And try not to gloat too much because it's liable to come back on you, brother."

"You don't have to worry about that. It's already on my doorstep." Brody settled his hat back on his head as he walked off.

Duke watched him go, wondering what in the world he meant by that. But he didn't really have time to think about his little brother's statement. After he had his own business settled, though, he'd get back to Brody.

His own business, meaning Oregon and Lilly. He remembered a Bible verse about not worrying because today's troubles were enough. Yeah, that was a paraphrase, but it made sense. No use borrowing trouble.

Chapter Fourteen

"We're going to do a biopsy."

Those hadn't been the words Oregon had expected to hear the doctor say on Wednesday. He'd scheduled tests that she thought would be noninvasive and would give them all of the answers they needed. But he wanted to go one step further.

She'd been alone when he gave her the news. Duke had taken Lilly for her appointment, and Oregon had insisted that there was no need for anyone to be with her.

When the procedure was over, she gathered her belongings and opened the door of the exam room. Duke was waiting in the hallway. He stepped away from the wall, tall and confident, an easy smile on his face. And suddenly she didn't feel so alone. Or as strong as she'd convinced herself she was.

"I should have been here." He stepped close and she leaned into his side. "Someone should have been here, Oregon."

"It wouldn't have changed anything, and Lilly needed you with her. Where is she?"

"She's in the waiting room. Joe and Sissy just got here. She's with them, getting quarters for the vending machine and probably having them sign the new cast."

"Why are they here?"

"Because they're your family. A person can only go through so much alone. After you texted me, I called them. They drove right up."

"I told you I could do this, Duke. It was just a biopsy."

He glanced down at her, shaking his head at what she'd meant to be a show of confidence on her part.

"We all know you can do everything on your own. I didn't want you to be alone, though. So I called and told them where to find you."

"Rat." She sniffed and turned away so he wouldn't see the tears in her eyes.

"You're going to be okay," he said with conviction.

"You promise?" She looked up, needing his

confidence. His fingers tightened around hers, and he lifted her hand to his lips.

She immediately regretted her words, though. She saw the shadows in his eyes and knew she'd brought back memories he'd tried so hard to vanquish, of soldiers pleading with him, asking him to save them, to promise they'd make it home.

"I'm sorry, that was wrong of me to ask you that."

He pulled her close to his side. "Don't apologize. Just know that I'm here and we're going to get through this."

She nodded at his reassurance. "I know. We should go."

They were almost to the exit when he pulled her to a stop. "I need for you to be okay." His voice shook as he said it.

"Me, too."

She held on to his hand, willing him to stay at her side. She'd never been that person, wanting to make a man stay. She wouldn't ask him to give what he couldn't. Emotion, thick and aching, settled in her throat. She was afraid. She didn't want to tell him that.

He muttered something, then gathered her in his arms as he moved her into an empty exam room. Tears leaked from her closed eyes as he held her close in that dark room. His mouth found hers, and she opened up to his kiss, needing to feel alive, to feel cherished in his arms. Even if it only lasted a moment, she needed to feel the connection.

As the kiss ended, he held her close against his chest. "We'll get through this."

"I know." She reached for a tissue and wiped her eyes. "We have to go. They'll probably charge us for using this room."

"It would be worth it."

When they entered the waiting room, Lilly, Joe and Sissy were waiting. Lilly sat next to Sissy, showing her something in a magazine. Joe seemed to be in prayer. Lilly saw them first, tossing the magazine and hurrying to Oregon's side.

"You're okay?" Lilly asked, her blue gaze shadowed with concern.

"I'm good. And look at that new cast. Nice." Oregon drew in a breath and let the fear go.

Lilly gave her a questioning look, then shifted her attention to the casted leg, obviously understanding they were playing a game of avoidance. "I can walk on it. And I'm doing so good they think it can come off in a few weeks."

"That's great. You'll be able to go swimming."

"Mom, you're going to be okay."

Was that a question or a statement of confidence? Oregon reached for her daughter's hand and held it tight. "Of course I'm going to be okay."

Lilly grinned big. "You know, as long as we're together, we can make it through anything."

"We always have."

Joe and Sissy were standing with them now. Joe patted her arm. "You're going to be just fine."

"Of course I am. And I'm ready to go home." She glanced around. "But my ride seems to have vanished."

"He went that way." Joe pointed to the door. "Lilly can wait here with us if you want to look for him."

"Thank you." Oregon kissed her daughter on the cheek. "Be right back."

She walked down the hall knowing there weren't too many places for Duke to go, unless he'd actually left. The women's clinic was attached to the hospital by a long hallway with few rooms. He wasn't in the next waiting room. He wasn't at the vending machine. She slowed at the door of the chapel and peeked in. He was sitting in a front pew, his head bowed.

She walked down the aisle and sat next to him. He placed his hand in hers.

"You disappeared." She leaned against him.

"I needed a minute alone, and I knew you were in good hands."

"Praying for me?" she asked softly.

"Praying for you, for me, for forgiveness." He leaned back, looking up at the ceiling. She wanted to brush away the worry from his face. She couldn't brush away his pain.

Duke held her hand in his and wished things could have been different for them both. He hadn't ever been much for wishing, though. He was an action man. That was the problem. He couldn't always fix the things he wanted to fix.

He had wanted to save every soldier he came across. Sometimes he couldn't, though. Too often he hadn't been able to do anything.

Once, a long time ago, he'd tried to make his mother come home. He'd been about eighteen when he chased her down. He'd told her it was too late for him, but she could get back to Texas and change things for Brody and Samantha. She'd told him she couldn't change anything for anyone, and they'd have to take care of themselves. What a piece of work Sylvia Martin was.

He wanted to tell Brody about that long-ago meeting with their mother, but it would tear him apart. Even a grown man sometimes needed to believe his mama cared a little bit.

A man needed to know that when he prayed for something important, God heard. He'd been down here pouring his heart out, begging forgiveness for all of that anger he'd carried back from Afghanistan. He'd been pleading for Lilly, that his little girl wouldn't have to know what life was like without a mom.

Duke liked to be in charge, to take care of things. He looked up at the cross on the wall of the chapel and felt a little bit humbled. He wasn't in this whole big mess alone.

He couldn't take care of everything and everyone. But he needed to know that God had this situation taken care of.

"Duke?" Oregon's voice called him back to the present.

"God's got this. Right?"

"I'd like to believe He does." She lifted his hand to her lips. The sweetness of the gesture shifted his whole world. "I wanted you in Lilly's life. I didn't mean to come barreling in with all of this extra baggage."

He pulled her close and kissed the top of her head. "All of this is part of being her dad. Being here for you means I'm here for her."

She stood, pulling his hand to bring him to his feet. "Lilly is probably worried about where we are."

"She's concerned, or maybe curious."

Before she could get away, he pulled her back into her arms and held her for just a moment.

Eventually she stepped away. "Lilly."

He nodded and followed her down the hall without telling her everything he wanted to say. Sometimes a man knew when to keep quiet.

He'd come to a few conclusions in that chapel. The first was that he had to be the man Oregon and Lilly needed. He was going to have to figure out who that man was, but he knew it started with faith. In time Oregon would see that God had made them a family. They had to do their part to become the family He wanted them to be.

Lilly met them in the hall. Her worried frown dissolved, and she smiled. "I thought maybe you left without me."

"Never." He pulled her close. No kid of his would ever feel walked out on. "I think if your mom is up to it, that we should grab something to eat."

"Drive-through?" Oregon asked. "Maybe we could take something home."

Home. When she said it like that, it sounded like a place they should be together. The three of them.

"I think that's a great idea. If Lilly is hungry, she can just eat on the way."

"I'm good. I've eaten half the stuff in the vending machine. And Joe," she said, glancing back at her grandfather who had just walked out of the waiting room, "Grandpa Joe bought me a sandwich earlier."

"Looks as if we can all head home, then," Duke said, moving them down the hall.

He eased an arm around Oregon. As they walked out the front doors, he stopped her. "Wait here and I'll go get the truck."

"I can walk to the truck, Duke." She started to follow after him but Joe stopped her, a restraining hand on her arm.

She huffed in frustration, then said, "I'll just wait here with you."

Duke headed toward the parking lot, liking Joe more than ever.

"Hey, could you slow down? I don't take giant steps."

He turned around and saw Lilly hurrying toward him. He slowed and she caught up. "Sorry." He pulled keys from his pocket. "You should have stayed with your mom."

"I wanted to be with my dad." She chewed on her bottom lip as she looked at him. "That's you."

"Yeah, that's me." They reached his truck and he stopped at the passenger door, stunned and unable to pull it together in order to give her more of an answer.

"So you're okay with me calling you that?"

He drew in a deep breath, then a grin burst across his face. He hugged her, lifting her off the ground. "I'm more than okay with it."

"Good. About my mom…"

He opened the truck door for her. She stood there, looking everywhere but at him. "You don't have to worry," he said.

She nodded but a finger came up, flicking away tears. His heart tightened a little. It was an uncomfortable feeling, like wearing new boots. He was suddenly Dad. The guy who needed to make her feel safe in all of these new situations crashing in on her.

"She's going to be fine. I'm going to make

sure of that. I'm not going anywhere and neither is she."

She fell into his arms, burying her face against his chest. Duke held her close as she sobbed. He brushed a hand down her head, smoothing her hair.

"It's okay."

She nodded against him, hiccuping on a sob. "I know."

"You can call me Dad anytime you want to." He was pretty close to tears himself at that moment. If she called him Dad right then, he'd be a goner.

"Okay."

He picked her up and sat her in the truck. "Seat belt."

She nodded and pulled the seat belt across her shoulder.

As they pulled through the circle drive, Oregon moved forward. Joe was still with her, his hand on her back. She said something and the two of them laughed. Joe patted her back and then reached for the door as Duke slowed to a stop.

"We'll see you back in Martin's Crossing," Duke called out to Joe.

"Not until tomorrow." Joe stood on the running board of the truck. "These two are tired.

Sissy will be there tonight if they need anything, but I'll have her drop me at my place."

"Good night, Joe." Oregon leaned to kiss his cheek.

Duke drove away from the hospital, Lilly and Oregon in the front seat of the truck with him. They went through a drive-through and were heading down the highway toward Martin's Crossing when he realized they were both asleep. He turned the radio down and settled in, his daughter against his shoulder and her mother leaning against the door.

The dogs, Daisy and Belle, met the truck as Duke pulled up to the house. He stopped the truck and got out. When he opened the passenger door, a groggy Oregon gave him a sweet, sleepy smile.

"We're home." She moved to get out. Before she could protest, he scooped her into his arms and carried her to the house. She was sleepy enough that she curled against him, her face in his neck, her breath soft and warm.

"I can walk," she whispered as they walked through the front door.

"Of course you can." He carried her inside and placed her on the couch. "But I liked carrying you, and I probably won't get many opportunities like that one."

She nodded, and then touched his face, cupping his cheeks with her hands. "No, and neither will I. It was nice."

"I'm going to get Lilly." He dropped a kiss on the top of Oregon's head. "Relax."

She reached for the quilt on the back of the sofa. "I will."

He stood there for a moment, watching as she dozed off again. When he turned, Lilly stood in the doorway watching. She looked at him, then at her mom.

"I don't want you to go," his daughter said in a quiet voice.

"I'm always going to be here, Lilly."

She shook her head. "I mean, don't leave us alone tonight, Dad. Please."

When she put it like that, he couldn't say no. He hugged her tight and nodded. "I'm not going anywhere."

Ever, he thought as he looked down at Oregon. He wasn't walking away from her, from them. He'd let her protest, let her turn him down, but he'd keep asking. He'd keep waiting for her to see what he had already realized.

They all belonged together.

Chapter Fifteen

The living room was washed in the gray light of early morning when Oregon woke up. She blinked a few times, stretched and sat up.

She definitely hadn't expected to sleep on the couch. A noise invaded early-morning stillness. A soft snoring from her favorite overstuffed chair. She smiled at the sight of Duke sprawled in the chair, his feet propped on the coffee table. He shouldn't have stayed. She would tell him that later. But she was glad he had. Even though Lilly was there and probably Sissy, it did her heart good to see that giant of a man, and to know he had kept watch through the night.

With quiet steps she got up and went to the kitchen. The least she could do was have coffee ready when he woke up. She started the coffeemaker, then she walked out the back door. The sun was just coming up, but it was already warm. In the distance she heard cattle. And faintly, from far away, the sound of a train blasting its horn through a crossing.

"You're up early."

She turned, smiling at Duke as he stepped out the door, brushing a hand through his hair. He looked sleepy but sweet. She wanted to lean into him and enjoy the sunrise. Instead, she focused away from him, on the field, the sun coming up, the cattle grazing.

"I can't believe I slept so long," she said over her shoulder. "And you probably didn't get enough sleep."

"I'm good on a few hours a night."

"I'm sure you are." She walked back to him and hugged him. "You are always there for us. When do we get to be there for you?"

His arms tightened around her. "This feels good. This is how you're here for me."

She wanted to agree, but she was suddenly afraid. It did feel good. Too good. Too right. Her heart felt bruised, vulnerable, fearful.

"Duke, what are we doing?"

"Right now?" He grinned as he said it. "We're holding each other."

"This situation."

"Oh yeah, that." He pulled away from her. "I should go."

"Duke, we have to talk."

"Yeah, I know we do. But I can tell by the tone you're using that you're not really ready to talk. You want to find a way to make this seem like the wrong thing to do. You want to tell me that I might walk out, or you can't have more children, all of the reasons we shouldn't be together."

"We do have to talk," she insisted.

He groaned, shaking his head. "Don't look at me like that. When you look at me that way, talking is the last thing I want to do. That look, all sweet and sleepy, makes me want to do this."

She started to ask what he meant, but her words were cut off as he claimed her lips in a softly insistent kiss. He held her close, brushing his lips against hers, kissing her slow and sweet. His hand held her close and as he raised his mouth from hers, he smiled a lazy smile that lingered in his blue eyes.

"That's why I need to go. Because we can't talk, and we can't do that. But that's what I want to do. I want to kiss you like that every single day for the rest of our lives."

She shook her head, unsure of what to say.

"I'm going to marry you, Oregon Jeffries. Not because we have a daughter, not that she isn't a good reason for us to get married, but because we belong together."

"Duke, I can't…"

"I knew you'd say that. I already told you all the excuses you'd make and I don't need to hear them again."

She shook her head. "You're not thinking logically."

"Sweetheart, I am always logical. I can promise you, if I'm proposing to a woman, then I mean it."

"But I'm not going to accept." She managed a light tone. "Go to the diner. I've kept you from your business, from your life, and it's time for you to get back to those things."

"You haven't kept me from anything. As a matter of fact, this Saturday, we're heading to a small rodeo. I promised Lilly I would ask if she could go."

"She can go."

"Thanks. And this discussion isn't over." His smile grew. "I'm going to keep asking until you say yes."

"Please, Duke, don't do that."

"Sorry, honey, I have to. I'm going to be

the man I'm supposed to be. That man prays, he trusts God and he's a husband and a dad."

"Go." Her voice unfortunately broke. Duke kissed her again, his hand gentle on her neck as his lips covered hers.

"Call if you need anything."

She nodded and watched him leave. When she walked through the back door, Sissy was sitting at the kitchen table with a cup of coffee. They were sisters but they were still basically strangers. And yet Sissy smiled as if they had always shared secrets over their morning coffee.

"You honestly told that man you won't marry him?"

Oregon poured herself a cup of coffee and grabbed a muffin left from the previous day. "He wants to take care of me, and he wants us to be a happy family."

"Eww, horrible," Sissy joked.

"Have you ever met a happy family?" Oregon asked.

"Yes, mine. And you've met happy families, too. You're just focused on your own unhappy experiences and refuse to believe that you might actually find a man and make a life that isn't dysfunctional."

"Pretty much." Oregon sat down across

from her sister. "I can't have children, and I might have cancer. Those are pretty big red flags."

"So when does life come with guarantees?" Sissy teased as she dunked cookies in her coffee.

"I wish it did." Oregon sighed and pushed the half-eaten muffin away. "Why does everything have to be so complicated?"

"Because in real life, things are complicated." Sissy grabbed both of their cups. "More coffee?"

Oregon nodded. "Please."

"Dad is going to ask you again to come to Dallas. Like your handsome prince, our father doesn't give up."

"I'm not getting married, and I'm not moving to Dallas." Oregon took the cup her sister handed her. "I need space."

"Maybe a vacation?"

"I wish I could. But I have a shop to run. I have a daughter."

"We have a condo in Florida."

At that, Oregon looked up. "We?"

"Our family, of which you are now a part. We have a condo in Florida. Beachfront. Why don't you take Lilly and go down there? I would come with you if you want."

She considered it. She really did. And then she shook her head. "I can't go."

"Of course not. You have a business. And a daughter. And a lot of excuses." Sissy pulled her chair close. "You have excuses why you can't let that gorgeous man into your life. You have excuses for why you can't go on vacation to the beach."

"I have responsibilities." Oregon chuckled because Sissy said the words with her. "You're very funny."

"I do my best. But if you change your mind about the condo, let me know. I can check the schedule and make sure no one is using it."

"Thank you. And now, I think I'll get ready and head for the shop. Would you like to go with us?"

"No, I have to make phone calls for Andrews Limited. Do you need me to do anything for you?" Sissy offered.

"Nothing that I can think of."

Oregon left a short time later. Lilly had chosen to stay home with the woman she was already calling Aunt Sissy. That meant Oregon was going to the shop alone. It meant realizing that as life changed, so did her relationship with her daughter. Lilly was gaining a family. A father. A grandfather. Aunts, uncles and cousins. She had those people to enjoy, to talk to, to spend time with.

Oregon had a man who wanted to marry her. But he hadn't mentioned love. And shouldn't love be a part of a marriage proposal?

Duke flipped burgers on the grill and called for Farris, his cook, to get fries and chicken strips going. Ned hurried through the door and grabbed the order he'd just finished.

"How's it going out there?" Duke asked as he flipped burgers onto plates where buns were waiting.

"Oh, it's a friendly mob, but nothing I can't handle. Aster is here. She's helping bus tables and fill drinks."

The teen girl who lived in town sometimes came in during lunch and dinner shifts to help keep things running smoothly. Ned said eventually she'd make a good waitress. Duke hoped so.

"How are you doing, boss?" Ned asked.

"Great. Thanks for asking. Do you have another order?"

"Nope, just wondering why you're cranky and look like something the dog dragged up to the porch."

Long night, but he didn't go into it with her. "I'm not cranky. Order up."

He rang the bell and pushed the plate down the counter.

"Not cranky at all." She cackled as she grabbed the plate and hurried out. "Oh, Boone Wilder is here."

"Send him back."

Boone walked through the kitchen door a minute later. He pushed his hat down tight on his head and leaned against the counter as Duke finished the latest order.

"You're a pretty good cook," Boone offered with a casual tilt of his lips.

"I'm glad you approve. Do you have another reason for being here?" Duke rang the bell again. Ned rushed through the door, grumbling that she was done for the day. He shook his head and pointed to the last plate of the daily lunch special. Open-faced roast beef.

"Yeah, I have a reason. Just waiting for a minute to share a few things with you." Boone grabbed a step stool and sat down.

Duke flipped a burger and chanced a look at the other man. Boone's expression didn't give a thing away.

"How's your business going?" Duke asked.

Boone shrugged. "Going. We're training,

advertising and hoping to open in the next six months. Why, you ready to give up cooking?"

"Not on your life."

The kitchen was empty. Duke waited.

"My friend came up with that other information you asked for," Boone finally said.

"Okay, so where's the info?"

Boone slid an envelope across the counter. "What are you going to do with that?"

"Not sure yet. Maybe just hold on to it."

"That'll get you in trouble."

"Probably, but what Brody doesn't know won't hurt him."

Boone shrugged again. "How's it going for Oregon and her family?"

"Good. Unless they convince her to leave town with them."

Boone pushed away from the counter. "If that happens, you can't blame me. You wanted them found."

"Right, I did want them found."

Boone left. Duke waited a few minutes and walked out to the dining room. Unfortunately Jake walked through the front door of the diner wearing a big grin that made Duke feel a little testy.

"Brother." Jake walked past him to the coffeepot and poured himself a cup.

"Sure, help yourself."

Jake lifted the cup. "Don't mind if I do. Brody told me about that fence the other day. I'm not sure what's going on but we had another section hit last night. Fortunately, I saw it and got it fixed before any cattle got out."

"What do you think is going on?" Duke poured himself a cup and sat across from his brother.

"Either kids or maybe someone out to steal some cattle. I told Brody we oughta do a head count."

Duke set his cup on the table. "Wouldn't be a bad idea."

"Mind helping us this evening? If we split up, it'll go a lot faster."

"Yeah, I can help. Let me go by and check on Oregon first."

"Shouldn't be a problem. She's at her shop."

"She should be at home, resting." He got up and crossed to the front door to look out.

"Hard to tell a woman what to do. And I doubt she feels like she has to check with you before she goes to work." Jake grinned as he said it and when Duke started to tell him what he thought of that, Jake lifted his cup and winked.

"Back off, Jake."

"Oh, I think I've given you plenty of slack. And it looks to me like you're doing a pretty bad job of dealing with this situation."

"There is no situation," Duke said. He sat back down and stretched to show he was relaxed. "Not a situation at all."

"None? That's hard for me to believe. How's Lilly? You should bring her out to the house again."

"I will."

"You going to marry Oregon?" Jake cut right to the chase.

"Get out." Duke stood up. "Just go because I'm not sitting here listening to this."

"I'm just worried about my little brother."

Duke stood, knowing he towered over Jake by several inches. "You don't have to worry about your little brother."

"Not at all?" Jake emptied his cup and stood. "Guess I'll go since you don't seem to want me around."

Duke shook his head. "I don't know what you're trying to pull, but I don't need this, not today."

"Let me guess." Jake leaned in close. "She said no."

"Yeah, she said no."

"What did you do wrong?"

"I asked her to marry me. How could I have done something wrong?"

"That's it? You just asked her to marry you? No flowers? No romance?"

"I didn't think…"

Jake laughed loud and long. "Obviously you didn't."

Duke walked away. Yeah, he'd had enough.

"If you need help, Mr. Ladies' Man…" Jake called out after him.

"I seem to recall that I helped you when you didn't know what to do with Breezy," Duke responded as he walked through the door to the kitchen.

He knew what he was doing. He'd just obviously done something wrong. It only made sense that they should get married. They should be a family.

Ned was waiting for him in the kitchen. Unfortunately, she looked like a woman with advice ready to give.

"What?" he asked on his way to the cooler.

"I didn't say anything."

"You want to," he called back over his shoulder. "You want to give me your two cents' worth."

"No, I really don't. But since you asked so nicely," she said in her growly voice, "you need to remember that she is going through a lot. She's just thirty, and in the last eighteen months she's fought cancer, lost the ability to have more children and then decided to share her daughter with you. That's a lot of loss. And before you say it, gaining you doesn't make up for everything."

"I wasn't going to say that."

Ned smirked at him from across the work-station. "But your big old ego was thinking it, boss. Just take my word for it, women like romance."

He popped an olive in his mouth. "I can do romance. Really, I can."

"You don't have a clue." Ned left the kitchen.

Duke let out a sigh, part relieved and part fed up. To himself he could admit, yeah, he was clueless. He could be charming when it suited his purposes.

But he obviously didn't know how to pro-pose. He was starting to wonder if he really knew anything about women.

Chapter Sixteen

Saturday evening Oregon drove her car through the gates of the rodeo grounds and found a parking space in the grass. Sissy had come along, after deciding to spend one more week getting acquainted. Joe had gone back to Dallas. It seemed strange to have him gone. She'd gotten used to his visits to her shop, to seeing him walking through town, helping at church. He'd assured her he'd be back from time to time. She knew it would change things. He would no longer be the mystery that no one could figure out. He would visit as her dad.

Joe was gone. And Lilly had gone to the rodeo with Duke.

Oregon took a deep breath and let it go. Tonight was about relaxing with her sister and forgetting that next week she would hear from the doctor's office concerning the biopsy.

"There's Duke and Lilly." Sissy pointed to the row of trucks and horse trailers at the back of the property.

Oregon turned off her car and sat for a moment. Sometimes she wondered if she was making a mistake, turning down his proposal. She'd never considered marrying. She'd never wanted to take the chance of someone walking out on her. What she couldn't explain to Duke was that the biggest reason she had for turning him down was Lilly. She didn't want her daughter to be collateral damage in their relationship. She didn't want Lilly to know the pain when someone walked away. Duke was wonderful but there were no sure things in life.

No matter what, she would protect her daughter.

She wouldn't let Lilly be her, always wondering if something would last or if it would end like everything else had ended. Her baggage, not her daughter's. She closed her eyes against the wave of past hurts.

"He's a sweet guy." Sissy's voice reached through the darker thoughts that had somehow taken hold.

Oregon smiled at her sister. "I know. A person wouldn't think that by looking at him, would they?"

"Maybe not. But he loves Lilly, and I think he'd do just about anything to make her happy."

"Yes, I think he would, too." Even marry her mother. She had to give him that. He was willing to give up his bachelor ways for Lilly's happiness.

He'd already done so much for them. He'd given them a home. He was in their lives, almost daily. He'd held Oregon when she needed to be held. His kisses made her feel as if she was still a whole woman.

She had to stop thinking that way. She was alive. She had a beautiful daughter. And her heart thought Duke Martin might be The One.

"Oregon, are you okay?"

Oregon nodded. "I'm good. Just need a moment."

"I understand."

They made their way to the trailer where Duke was saddling his big gray gelding. The horse stomped at the flies buzzing his legs and turned his head to nip at his side. Duke pushed his head back and gave the girth strap a pull. The horse stomped his back leg and turned that big head to nip at Duke's sleeve.

"Listen, Animal, I've had enough of your bad manners." Duke pushed the horse's head back again. Lilly, sitting on a nearby lawn chair, laughed. Duke winked at his daughter, then he gave a slight nod to Oregon and Sissy.

Oregon watched her daughter and Duke as they joked and laughed while he finished up with his horse. Watching them, it was obvious they were becoming a father and daughter. And from the way he wasn't looking at her, it was obvious that maybe he'd taken her at her word and was giving her space.

Next to her Sissy whistled. Oregon looked at her, surprised by the uncharacteristic gesture from someone who normally seemed so composed.

"What was that?" Oregon asked.

Sissy turned a little pink. "I…well… There." She pointed to a cowboy a few trailers down. His blond hair was a little longer than average, and his jeans were holey. He grinned their way, and Oregon was sure he winked.

"That's trouble, if you ask me," Duke said as he reached to untie his horse. "His name is Dale Trueblood, and he's been in more trouble than I can list."

Sissy didn't seem fazed.

Brody joined them a few minutes later, limping but happier than Oregon had seen him in the past six months or so. He grinned, tipping his hat in greeting.

"You're not riding bulls tonight, are you?" Oregon asked.

"Nope. My bull-riding days are over." He patted Duke's horse on the rump. "I'm just here to help. I'm not even doing any roping."

Oregon looked from Brody to Duke. Duke just shrugged. "I'm going to warm this guy up."

She watched him go and tried to tell herself that this distance between them was what she wanted. If that was true, then why did it hurt so much?

With a lot of effort, she managed to smile at her sister.

"We should go find seats. Lilly, are you going with us?"

She already knew the answer to that question. Lilly would stay with Duke and watch the rodeo from back here. Oregon knew it wouldn't be long before Lilly would be here on a horse of her own. But Lilly would have more than one summer of playing cowgirl. That thought lightened Oregon's mood.

"I'm staying. Is that okay? I mean, I could sit with you."

"No, you stay here with your dad." Oregon hugged her daughter tight and then let go. Because that's what a mom did. They learned to let go. Children grew up, and letting go was part of the process.

"Thanks, Mom. I love you."

"Love you, too." Oregon walked away, fighting the tears that were also a part of letting go.

Sissy bumped a shoulder against Oregon's. "She's a great kid."

"Yes, she is."

"Duke isn't taking her. He's just filling in the place where a dad belongs."

Oregon looked at her younger sister. "You are great to have around. Thank you."

They found Breezy in the bleachers with the twins. Rosie and Violet waved and started to jabber as soon as they saw Oregon. Oregon sat next to Breezy, Violet on her lap, Sissy on her other side. Across the arena she could see the trailer where Lilly waited for Duke. She saw him ride up on the horse named Animal. He leaned down and a moment later, Lilly appeared in the saddle behind him.

She hugged Violet tight. This was her family. And it worked.

Duke pulled back on the reins and glanced over his shoulder at his daughter. "You good back there?"

"I'm good." She grabbed the sides of his shirt when Animal side-hopped a little. "He's a big horse."

"He is, but he's not going to do anything he shouldn't. He might act a little ornery, but he knows he has to obey."

"I trust you."

Those words went straight to his heart. His daughter trusted him.

"Is your mom in the stands?" He rode up to the arena.

She nodded against his shoulder but held on tight.

A young woman rode to the center and faced the crowds. She held the American flag high, and the crowds stood for the national anthem. Duke removed his hat and held it to his chest. It didn't matter how many times he heard it and took part in the ceremony, or how old he got—the song and what it meant moved him.

He'd seen that flag fly over lands where

some people would just as soon blow it up as look at it. And yet the flag still flew, and brave men and women still fought for freedom. Freedom for other people, other lands. Yeah, that meant a lot.

When that song played, he didn't care who saw the tears in his eyes.

After the national anthem, there was a prayer. And then it was time for the rodeo. Duke put his hat back on his head, pushing it down a little. People in the stands cheered. Animal stomped his mammoth-sized hooves and swung his head, ready for some calf roping.

"Do you want me to let you off here so you can join your mom?" he asked Lilly before he turned the horse back toward the trailer.

"Yeah, sure."

He took her arm and let her slide to the ground. True to form, Animal stood as still as a statue. The big horse might act up once in a while, but he knew when to be serious. Lilly rubbed the horse's head and smiled up at Duke.

"Someday I'm going to ride him," she announced with a confident look. And he didn't doubt it.

"Someday. But not until you've been riding your own horse a little while."

"Deal." She waved, then headed for her mom in the stands. He scanned the crowd and spotted Oregon. He raised a hand to the brim of his hat and tipped his head. She waved, but then Breezy said something and she looked away.

He turned Animal and headed for Jake, Brody and a group of locals who were standing together looking at a horse. He rode up next to Brody. Duke tried to remember the last time he'd seen his brother on a horse.

"What's going on?" Duke asked.

"Jim Bailer is selling this mare. He said he doesn't need her now that his daughter is married."

Duke looked the mare over and nodded. "Nice horse. You going to buy her?"

"Nope."

"When was the last time you got on a horse?"

"Can't remember." Brody started to walk away. Duke followed on Animal. "You can stop following me."

Duke reined his horse in and swung to the ground. "I'm not following. I'm walking the same direction."

"You have a kid. I'm not that kid. If you want to give me a break, that would be good."

"Brody, she doesn't want to be found." The words slipped out, not at all what he was planning to say.

Brody spun around and stared him down. "Just because your life is messed up, and you can't seem to make a woman give you the time of day, doesn't mean you have to stick your nose in my business."

"This isn't your business, Brody, it's all of ours. Sylvia Martin isn't interested in being a mother. Finding her won't change that."

"How do you know?" Brody took off his hat and swept a hand through his dark hair.

"Because I found her once about fourteen years ago. She laughed and told me I was wasting my time trying to drag her back to this one-horse town and a bunch of ungrateful…" He stopped but he should have quit talking a little sooner. Brody wasn't a kid, but he was still that little boy that Sylvia Martin had left when he still needed her to tuck him in at night.

"You should have told me." Brody's voice was low, steady, controlled. "I deserved to know."

"You were twelve, and Sam was nine. I

wanted Sylvia back for your sakes. I wasn't about to tell you that she wouldn't come."

"Where is she now?"

Duke shook his head. "Who really knows or cares?"

From the look on his face, he knew the answer to that question. Brody cared. At twenty-six, he still cared. He thought about his own daughter and how she might have grown up not knowing him, always wondering who he was and where he was.

Oregon had made sure their daughter didn't go through that.

"Brody, I'm sorry." He reached for his brother's arm.

Brody shook him off and shot him an angry glare. "I don't need your apologies. I'm going to find her. She's going to explain to me how she could walk out on her kids."

At that, Brody marched away. Duke swung himself back into the saddle and watched him go. He didn't know how to fix this, how to make things better for his brother.

Promise me she'll come back, Duke.

Brody had made him promise that over twenty years ago. And Duke had promised because he'd been a kid, too. He'd wanted to make his little brother feel better about being tucked in by him, letting him believe their mother would come back someday and resume her place in their lives.

Another promise he hadn't kept.

Why did promises make him think of Oregon Jeffries in the stands with his daughter? Maybe because he couldn't remember if he had made her promises thirteen years ago. Did this rodeo remind her of the night they first met?

Had he promised to look her up? Instead, he'd blacked out and forgotten everything, including her face, her name and the fact that he might have a baby on the way.

He had a lot of regrets, and at that moment, what he'd done to her was at the top of the list.

She deserved a man who wouldn't let her down. He was going to be that man. Or die trying.

Chapter Seventeen

Monday and Tuesday passed without hearing from the doctor's office. By Wednesday Oregon was going insane. She had said goodbye to Sissy that morning, the two of them promising to visit each other often. After Sissy left, Lilly hurried across the street to Duke's.

That had become their routine. Oregon went to work each morning at her shop. Lilly went to Duke's and spent time with him. Usually around noon, she showed up at Oregon's shop with lunch for them both. Oregon needed to tell Duke that he didn't have to feed her. It had become his habit, to feed her lunch. Sometimes in the evenings she got home from work to find dinner in the oven or in the slow cooker.

Not that she complained much. Duke was a better cook than she was.

But she wasn't his responsibility. That's what she needed for him to understand. Before he attempted another proposal, she had to make him understand. To Duke Martin she was just another responsibility. She was a promise he thought he could keep. He could take care of them, make them feel safe, provide for them.

For some silly reason tears slid down her cheeks. Hormones. She brushed at the dampness and went back to work on the Christmas ornaments she needed to paint. Yes, Christmas was six months away. But people would start buying ornaments in October. She wanted to have a surplus.

The phone rang. She reached for it, her hand shaking, her heart painfully thumping in her chest. She answered, waited, listened to the nurse on the other end. And then she said a polite "thank you" and dropped the phone. Tears blurred her vision, and she couldn't think. She needed air. She needed to breathe. She stood and when she started for the back door, she saw Duke, a Styrofoam container in his hand. He didn't move.

"I need to go outside," she said as tears rolled down her cheeks. "Where's Lilly?"

"She's at the diner with Ned's niece." He put

the container down on a table and reached for her. She couldn't let him touch her, not yet. "Oregon?"

She shook her head and kept walking. "Give me a minute."

He followed her to the back room where she stopped at the screen door. Duke touched her shoulder, and she wanted to fall into his embrace and let him hold her. But she wouldn't fall apart. She didn't have to fall apart. She took a deep, shaky breath.

"I'm cancer-free."

He pulled her close. She could hear his heart pounding, and she felt him sigh loudly.

"We're going to celebrate tonight." He continued to hold her. "Steaks on the grill. My place."

"You don't have to."

"I want to." He raised her hand to his lips and held it there. "I need to."

Oregon looked up, unsure of what she saw in his eyes. Whatever it was, it scared her. Thrilled her. Made her want to stay and figure it out. But she knew she shouldn't. What connected them was Lilly. And that wasn't enough. Not for her. Not when she knew her heart wanted more from him. She wanted the whole package. She wanted love and forever with this man.

She didn't want promises to be there for her. She didn't want this to be about not letting them down. She wanted his heart, his love.

And she hadn't allowed herself to think about that before because fear had held her back, making her only think about keeping Lilly secure.

"Oregon, please, come to dinner. Lilly and I will head home at five and get everything ready."

For some reason she nodded. She had planned on telling him she couldn't, she had other things to do. Instead, she said she would be there.

"Your lunch is in there. Don't forget to eat." He leaned, brushing a kiss across her lips. She closed her eyes, wishing. But what good did wishing do?

"Thank you. And you can tell Lilly for me, okay?"

"I will. She hasn't said anything, but I know she's been worried."

Oregon nodded in agreement and watched him go. After he left she gave herself a good lecture for accepting his invitation. She should have said no. From now on she would say no.

They would have to figure out how to parent together without letting the lines get smudged.

Father. Mother. Daughter. But not a family.

Duke heard the car door slam, and then Daisy barked a greeting, not a warning. It would be Oregon. He hadn't invited her here before. There hadn't been a reason not to; they had just always met at the cottage.

When he met her at the door she handed him a bottle of sparkling juice. He took the gift and leaned to kiss her cheek. He fought the urge to do more, to pull her close and kiss her. It wasn't time for that. Not yet.

"Where's Lilly?" Oregon stepped into the living room and looked around. "This is nice. I really wasn't expecting shabby chic in a bachelor home."

He grinned as he looked around the living room with the painted wood floors and over-stuffed furniture he'd gotten cheap second-hand. "I didn't know the style, just knew that it was comfortable."

"And my daughter?"

"She's with Breezy and Jake."

"But she was supposed to be here, too, wasn't she?"

"Oregon, I wanted tonight to be about us."

"Us?" she whispered. "Duke, there is no us. We have a daughter together, but…"

If she kept going, he wouldn't have a chance. He took her by the hand and led her to the kitchen. White painted cabinets, dark countertops that were almost indestructible and French doors that led to the deck. He hadn't really thought about it when he'd been remodeling and finishing things up over the past month, but it had become a family home, a place where a couple could raise a kid or two and be happy.

Lately he'd been thinking a lot about them in this house together. He'd thought about Oregon when he knocked out a wall between two bedrooms to create a master suite with a sitting room.

He'd thought about her as he stocked the kitchen, as he finished the library. He'd been thinking about her a lot.

"Something smells good."

He grinned. "Homemade cheesecake."

"I love cheesecake. But why did you take up cooking? I mean, I see you outside with horses and cattle. But cooking?"

"You think a rancher can't make a mean cheesecake, or grill up an amazing steak?"

He opened the oven door and pulled out the cheesecake.

"It fits you. The diner fits you. But why did you decide to come home and open a diner?"

He leaned against the counter and studied the woman at the table. Some things just didn't make sense. Like how, all of a sudden, he couldn't think of a day without her in it.

"When I got home from Afghanistan, I started drinking again. Marty, the housekeeper we've had for years, put a stop to that. She said she'd dragged me out of the bottle once, and I wasn't going back in. So she put me to work in the kitchen with her. Kneading bread. Great therapy."

"She's a great lady. I think Joe has taken her out to dinner a few times."

"I think he has. And I couldn't agree more that she's great. After I got sober, I moved into the cottage and started renovating this place. And I baked. I cooked. It helped me sort my thoughts and get my head on straight. It helped me stay sober. That's why I bought the old diner and opened Duke's."

"I understand. I do what I do because when I was a teenager, art and sewing were things I could take with me wherever I went. No matter what kind of crazy existence my mom wanted, I had a refuge in art."

Duke opened the door to the deck. Heat flowed in. "I'm going to turn the steaks. Baked potatoes and salad are ready. I have a loaf of French bread warmed up."

"What can I do?"

He shrugged and smiled down at her. Her gray eyes locked with his, wary, unsure. "Keep me company."

She followed him outside. Duke turned the steaks and glanced at his watch. "Six more minutes."

Oregon moved to his side. Her gaze flicked to the field and then to him. "Duke, I need to know what's going on."

Duke glanced at his watch again. Sometimes things didn't go the way a man planned. He could time it to perfection, have it all organized, then a string got pulled and everything unraveled.

A month ago he never would have pictured himself in this moment with her.

"Oregon, I want to marry you." He tipped her chin so that she looked up at him. "I want to have a life with you and with my daughter."

"I can't. Duke, I can't do this."

He had expected that. He'd planned for it.

"I think you've convinced yourself you can't. I think you have ideas about being a woman, about being whole and about having more children. I understand all of those doubts you've bottled up and held on to. But I'm telling you, Oregon Jeffries, I want to marry you."

She shook her head and walked away.

That was something he hadn't planned.

Chapter Eighteen

Oregon walked through the house, no longer noticing the pretty furniture, the wonderful aromas or even how her feet moved one in front of the other. Her heart ached and she needed to escape.

Or stay and be the woman that Duke Martin loved. But he hadn't mentioned love. He'd said they should be together. They should be a family. And she agreed. They would make a wonderful family. But there were so many factors. There were so many doubts.

Past hurts were chasing her down, causing her fear. Insecurity doubled its efforts to keep her from reaching for what she wanted. She wanted Duke in her life. She wanted to wake up every morning knowing that he would be there, loving them and protecting them.

She wanted to believe he would be the man who wouldn't walk out when things got tough. She wanted to believe in those vows, the ones that promised to have and to hold forever. The little girl in her remembered her mother standing with too many men making those same promises. And each time the girl Oregon had been wished that this time would be real, this time they would stay.

The front door opened. Duke joined her on the porch where she'd stopped, unable to keep running. She wouldn't run from him anymore, from her feelings or her fears.

She would confront this head-on and tell him why it wouldn't work.

She closed her eyes and prayed, because God had gotten her through so much. He would get her through this. He would help her face today without holding on to the past and the things she couldn't change.

"I'm sorry. I shouldn't have asked you that way." Duke's hand was on her shoulder.

"I can't have more children." The words weren't the ones she really meant to say. She'd meant to tell him she couldn't marry him. Instead, those words that had ached inside her since last year had spilled out. She covered her face with her hands.

Duke's arms encircled her. He kissed the top of her head. "I'm sorry. It's been a rough few weeks. I know that you would give anything to have more children."

"I hadn't ever thought about it before. I had Lilly, and I love her, and she was enough. She is enough."

"Of course she is. But things change. People change and so do circumstances."

She nodded, still safe in his arms. A little voice told her to move, to not get too comfortable. But she couldn't move. She couldn't stop needing him.

His lips brushed hers, then claimed them in a kiss that stopped her from thinking about doubt and fear. His kiss filled her up and made her feel every bit a woman. His hand slid from her shoulder to the back of her neck. Oregon held on to his arms, needing his strength. She sobbed as the kiss lingered.

"Oh, Duke, don't do that to me." She whispered the words against his arm, kissing him on the exposed skin of his forearm.

"Do what? Make you want to say yes?"

She heard the smile in his words, and when she looked up, his blue eyes twinkled with amusement and victory.

"Yes. I mean, no." She shook her head and

burrowed into the comfort of his chest. "I can't think."

"That's my plan. I want you not thinking about anything other than how right this is."

"Duke, this isn't enough for a marriage. Yes, we have Lilly, and we have chemistry. But I want more. I want to be loved." She bit down on her bottom lip to keep from saying more but it couldn't be held back. "Because I love you."

Duke cupped her cheeks in his hands and kissed her again, a long, lingering kiss. After a sweet kiss and then brushing his lips across her cheek, he reached for her hand. Before she could stop him, he dropped to one knee. Still holding her hand, he took his hat off.

"Don't ever leave me, Oregon Jeffries. I have this problem." He cleared his throat, and he grinned. "When you're around, I can't think straight. You've taken away my ability to think like a confirmed bachelor. It's no longer all about me. It's about us. It's about you, me and our daughter. And if she's it for us, then that's pretty great because not everyone is as blessed. Thirteen years ago, I messed up. But I wasn't much of a man back then. I definitely wouldn't have been man enough to take care of you and our baby."

"Duke, stand up."

"No, I'm going to do this right." He remained on one knee.

"Okay, then, I'm coming down here with you." Oregon joined him, going down on both knees in front of him. It felt better there, close to him.

He kissed her again. She could get used to those kisses.

"Oregon, we have a second chance. I can't help but believe that God meant that to happen. I can't deny it took me by surprise. I definitely had no intentions of falling in love."

He paused there.

"But?" she prompted, needing the words so desperately that it didn't make sense.

"I have this strange malady. I can't stop thinking about the mother of my daughter. I think that's the way it should be. I can't sleep at night, and it isn't because of nightmares. It's because I'm constantly thinking about when I can see you again, or hold you, or kiss you. I love you, and I want to marry you."

Duke gave up leaning on one knee. Oregon sat down in front of him. He pulled her close to his side and leaned against the post at the edge of the porch. Once again, so much for his great romantic plans. He hadn't expected the two of them on their knees on the front porch.

"Oregon?"

She moved, going to her knees next to him. She brushed her hand across his cheek, and he closed his eyes. Man, she was the sweetest thing ever. When she looked at him like that, he'd give her anything she asked for.

"I'm afraid. I want this. I want you. I want marriage and a family. And I'm scared to death it won't last. As afraid as I am for myself, I'm more afraid for Lilly and what that would do to her."

"We are not our parents." He opened his eyes, needing for her to see that truth reflected in his expression. "I have never told a woman I love her. I've never thought about asking one to marry me. I'm not a kid, Oregon. I know what I want. I want you."

"I want you, too."

"I didn't think a proposal would feel like a debate." He smoothed dark hair back from her face. "I've seen it done in movies and when the guy asks, the woman generally cries and says yes."

"The man usually starts with the words *I love you*, so she knows he's serious."

He laughed at that. "You have a point. Should I start over?"

"Maybe."

"If I do, will you say yes? Because if I'm going to have to eat cold steak, I'd at least like to know that something went right tonight."

She stood and reached for his hand to pull him to his feet. He found that amusing, that her pint-size self thought she could help him up. He took her hand, though.

This time he did what he should have done from the beginning. He reached into his pocket and pulled out the ring he'd bought a week ago. It had been Breezy's idea, to be prepared with a big diamond. Girls love diamonds, even when they say they don't, she'd told him.

He wasn't going down on one knee again, though. Instead, he reached for her left hand, and he held it for a minute, studying her beautiful fingers, feeling the pulse in her wrist. He lifted that wrist to his lips and planted a kiss where he could feel the beat of her heart.

"Oregon Jeffries," he started with a wink, "I love you. I love our daughter. And I would love for you to marry me and be my wife. I promise we're going to be together and be there for each other and for our daughter." He leaned toward her. "Was that better?"

Tears rolled down her cheeks. "That was perfect. Yes, Duke, I'll marry you."

"I thought you'd never say yes." He picked her up and swung her around. And he kissed her as he held her, refusing to let her feet touch the ground.

He said a quiet prayer of thanks, because God had seen exactly what they needed. They had needed each other. Broken hearts, broken lives, and now they were whole.

Epilogue

Christmas, two years later

Oregon left the shop early, flipping the Open sign to Closed. Her heart was almost giddy, as if she was sixteen and going on her first date.

But it wasn't. It was a Christmas tree she had an appointment with. She drove home as fast as the speed limit and traffic allowed. Duke's truck was parked in the driveway of their house. He waved from the ladder where he was hanging lights. December first. It had been their tradition since they got married on Christmas two years earlier to hang lights on the first of December.

This year they were starting new traditions. She parked her car and stepped out. Duke came down the ladder and met her. He pulled her close and whispered in her ear. She laughed and kissed him back.

"You are very bad, Duke Martin."

"Only with you, Mrs. Martin." He curved an arm around her waist.

The front door opened and banged shut. "Break it up. Break it up."

Lilly smiled at the two of them. She wore shorts and a T-shirt. Silly Texas weather. Didn't it know enough to be cold in December? At this rate they wouldn't even be able to have a fire in the fireplace tonight when they decorated the tree.

"We refuse to break it up," Duke told her. "But you can give your old dad a hug, then help him string lights."

Lilly hurried down off the steps. The front porch had been decorated with holly and in honor of the holidays, the cushions on the wicker furniture had been changed to red and green. Lilly gave Daisy and Belle each a quick pat before grabbing lights to hand up to Duke as he climbed the ladder.

"What time will they be here?" Lilly asked.

"Soon, I think." Oregon looked down the road.

"You're sure they're coming?"

"They're coming. Mrs. Flanders called and said they'd be here at five."

"So we have an hour to decorate." Duke hung lights on the plastic holders.

"Yes." Oregon watched from the safety of the ground. "Did you test to make sure these work?"

"They work."

She repeated the question. Duke frowned. Because he hadn't tested the lights. That, too, was a Martin family tradition. Duke never tested the lights unless Oregon reminded him.

"I'll test them," Oregon offered.

"That's why I love you."

"Enough mush," Lilly said, unstringing more lights. "I think I included that in the vows at the wedding. No mush, no sweet-talking in front of the kid."

Oregon plugged in the lights and held her breath. When the red bulbs twinkled along the strand, she breathed a sigh of relief.

"Oh, you of little faith," Duke called down from his perch on the ladder.

"I hear a car." Lilly turned to watch the drive, and Oregon waited.

"False alarm."

Duke finished stringing the lights. He'd already wrapped lights around the six support posts on the porch. Oregon finished the posts off with red ribbons. They were standing back, surveying a job well-done, when a car did come down the road and turn into the driveway.

Oregon reached for his hand, and he squeezed. "It's going to be great, Oregon."

"I know it is."

Lilly slid between the two of them, and they wrapped their arms around her as they waited. The front door of the car opened. Mrs. Flanders stepped out. She waved and then opened the back door of her sedan. Duke, Oregon and Lilly went forward.

Mrs. Flanders unbuckled a car seat in the back of her car. She pulled out a sleepy little girl of about two. The child, whose name was Maria, held pudgy arms out to Oregon. Dark hair framed her sleepy face, but her eyes locked on Duke, and she grinned.

"Dute."

"Yeah, baby, I'm Dute. You can call me whatever you want as long as you look at me with those brown eyes." Duke held out his arms, and she left Oregon's embrace for his.

Lilly had taken the next child from Mrs. Flanders. A little boy with chestnut-brown hair and coffee-colored eyes. "And here is

Mr. Bobby." The caseworker smiled as the boy grabbed hold of Lilly, his thumb in his mouth.

"I would have been here sooner, but we had to stop for milk." Mrs. Flanders tickled the little boy who had gone from Lilly to Oregon. "Didn't we, bossy man?"

Bobby grinned. His thumb remained in his mouth, but he put his free arm around Oregon's neck. She cuddled against him, inhaling the sweet scent of baby powder and soap.

"Have they eaten?" Oregon asked.

"We had a late lunch and they had crackers, as you can see, in my car. Bobby is a little underweight, so he's still on formula. The foster mom sent you letters about their eating and sleeping habits. She also sent photo albums. She's so thrilled for you all and so thankful that you'll let her visit."

"Of course we will. She'll be a special part of their lives." Oregon held the little boy that would soon be hers. One more court date, and they would be a family of five. Duke wrapped an arm around her and pulled her close. Lilly, thrilled to be a big sister, started grabbing bags and boxes.

"Would you like some coffee?" Duke asked

the caseworker as they walked through the front door.

"I'd love a cup of coffee," Mrs. Flanders answered.

The tree was up in the corner and lit. Duke had piled boxes of decorations nearby. Maria's eyes lit up, and she patted his cheek.

"Tree," the little girl whispered.

Duke let her down, and she toddled to the tree, touching the branches and then pulling back. She giggled and turned to look at them. She was theirs. Oregon's heart filled to over-flowing.

God had done this. He'd led them to these children who would have a permanent home with them. It didn't surprise her. After all, when God made the plan, it was perfect.

She looked from Lilly to Duke, to the two children that were now a part of their lives. Her gaze traveled to the photographs on the wall of Lilly growing up, of a wedding with the three of them together, and soon there would be pictures of five.

Oregon shifted Bobby to her left arm. "I'll be back with that cup of coffee."

She carried Bobby to the kitchen and placed him in the new high chair they'd bought.

As she put a cup under the spout of the

coffeemaker and pushed a button, a hand slid around her waist and rough whiskers brushed her cheek. Duke leaned in from behind her, pulling her against his chest.

"I love you, Mrs. Martin."

"I love being Mrs. Martin," she returned with a grin she tossed back at him.

He laughed and brushed his cheek against hers again. "You're supposed to say you love me back."

"I love you back, Duke."

And then a little voice behind them said "Dute" and giggled.

* * * * *

Dear Reader,

I hope you enjoy the second book in the Martin's Crossing series. I loved Duke and Oregon from the moment they walked onto the pages of *A Rancher for Christmas*. This couple has learned from experience that life isn't always perfect. Sometimes it's messy. People can't always be who we need them to be. In *The Rancher Takes a Bride*, Duke and Oregon take a chance and what they find is beautiful. They learn to trust, and they put aside their own fears in order to do what is right for a child who desperately needs them both. In the process they find a love that binds them all together.

Be sure to look for Duke's brother Brody's book, coming in Fall 2015.

Hope you enjoyed your time in Martin's Crossing!

Brenda Minton

LARGER-PRINT BOOKS!

GET 2 FREE
LARGER-PRINT NOVELS
PLUS 2 FREE
MYSTERY GIFTS

Love Inspired®
SUSPENSE
RIVETING INSPIRATIONAL ROMANCE

Larger-print novels are now available...

YES! Please send me 2 FREE LARGER-PRINT Love Inspired® Suspense novels and my 2 FREE mystery gifts (gifts are worth about $10). After receiving them, if I don't wish to receive any more books, I can return the shipping statement marked "cancel." If I don't cancel, I will receive 4 brand-new novels every month and be billed just $5.49 per book in the U.S. or $5.99 per book in Canada. That's a savings of at least 19% off the cover price. It's quite a bargain! Shipping and handling is just 50¢ per book in the U.S. and 75¢ per book in Canada.* I understand that accepting the 2 free books and gifts places me under no obligation to buy anything. I can always return a shipment and cancel at any time. Even if I never buy another book, the two free books and gifts are mine to keep forever.

110/310 IDN GH6P

Name _____ (PLEASE PRINT) _____

Address _____ Apt. # _____

City _____ State/Prov. _____ Zip/Postal Code _____

Signature (if under 18, a parent or guardian must sign)

Mail to the **Reader Service:**
IN U.S.A.: P.O. Box 1867, Buffalo, NY 14240-1867
IN CANADA: P.O. Box 609, Fort Erie, Ontario L2A 5X3

**Are you a current subscriber to Love Inspired® Suspense books
and want to receive the larger-print edition?
Call 1-800-873-8635 or visit www.ReaderService.com.**

* Terms and prices subject to change without notice. Prices do not include applicable taxes. Sales tax applicable in N.Y. Canadian residents will be charged applicable taxes. Offer not valid in Quebec. This offer is limited to one order per household. Not valid for current subscribers to Love Inspired Suspense larger-print books. All orders subject to credit approval. Credit or debit balances in a customer's account(s) may be offset by any other outstanding balance owed by or to the customer. Please allow 4 to 6 weeks for delivery. Offer available while quantities last.

Your Privacy—The Reader Service is committed to protecting your privacy. Our Privacy Policy is available online at www.ReaderService.com or upon request from the Reader Service.

We make a portion of our mailing list available to reputable third parties that offer products we believe may interest you. If you prefer that we not exchange your name with third parties, or if you wish to clarify or modify your communication preferences, please visit us at www.ReaderService.com/consumerschoice or write to us at Reader Service Preference Service, P.O. Box 9062, Buffalo, NY 14240-9062. Include your complete name and address.

LISLP15